D0264795

HOW

HOW THEY CHOSE THE DEAD

HOW THEY CHOSE THE DEAD

Stories by HOLLIS SUMMERS

LOUISIANA STATE UNIVERSITY PRESS
BATON ROUGE 1973

ISBN 0-8071-0221-0
Library of Congress Catalog Card Number 72-94153

Manufactured in the United States of America
Printed by The Colonial Press Inc., Clinton, Massachusetts
Designed by Albert Crochet

The stories in this volume appeared originally in the following publications and are reprinted with their permission: *New World Writing, Sewanee Review, New Voices, Red Clay Reader, Quarterly Review of Literature, Accent, Epoch, Colorado Quarterly, Paris Review, Hudson Review,* and *Fresco.*

For Bunny and Jack

Contents

HOW
THEY
CHOSE
THE
DEAD

How They Chose the Dead

Margaret stuck one candle in the middle of Chip's birthday cake, and I lit it with my cigarette lighter. "Blow, blow, Chip," Margaret said.

But Chip didn't blow. He just held the new plastic ball with both hands and banged it against the tray of his highchair. The bell inside the ball tinkled and Chip laughed. Margaret and I laughed too.

"It's wonderful, isn't it?" I said.

"It's wonderful," Margaret said. She leaned against the sink and watched Chip bang the ball. "He won't ever die, will he? He's so beautiful."

The ball slipped from Chip's hand and clinked onto the floor. It didn't roll far. It only wobbled and the bell rang inside it.

"Damn," I said, and Chip said something that sounded like damn, and then he said, "Car-car."

He never did get the idea of blowing out the candle. Once during lunch he put his chin in the icing and drew back as if he'd been burned. We laughed at that too. The frosting was like lather on his face; he licked his lips and laughed with us and said, "Car-car."

"Chip wants to take a long, long ride," Margaret said. "That's what you want, isn't it, Chip? For a birthday present."

Chip banged the blue plastic ball and the bell rang and we got ready to take the long, long ride. I put Chip's mattress in the back of our coupé. I covered the mattress with a sheet and tucked in the corners as if it were a hospital bed. Margaret fixed part of the birthday dinner for a picnic. She had fried chicken and the first tomatoes from our garden and cans of liver and spinach and custard. "And he'll have cake for dessert," Margaret said. "Cake, Chip, you hear that?"

She forgot the diapers and we had to turn around at the edge of town and come back. I wasn't even annoyed with her for forgetting, and she said that I drove better than she did.

"I'm glad we got to see our house again anyhow," Margaret said. "I'm not sorry about leaving the diapers."

"It's a beautiful house," I said.

Chip stood up on his mattress and pressed his face against the back window. He beat the blue ball against the glass.

"Chip's glad we came back. He never heard of its being bad luck."

The motor of the car sounded good. I was listening to the motor. "It's never been bad luck," I said after a minute. "And we're always forgetting things."

"I love you," Margaret said. "I love you and Chip."

"I love you and Chip." I rolled the window up so that there wouldn't be too much air in the back.

Neither of us has any idea how far we drove. I keep trying to visualize the mileage numbers under the speedometer, but nothing comes. We know, of course, that we passed through Carrollton, and that's twenty-three miles from home. It was just two o'clock in Carrollton. The clock over the courthouse said so.

I said, "It's time for his nap, isn't it?"

And Margaret said, "You don't have naps on your birthday, you ought to know that."

Chip came over in the front seat with us. He sat between us and began a lot of talk without words. He didn't look sleepy.

I drove around the courthouse a couple of times and then turned right and went over a bridge. We're both sure we went over a bridge, even though we didn't think anything about it at the time. In a little while we hit a macadam road that had sugar maples along the sides. The road was a cave. The sun shone through the leaves and ran ahead of us. I don't remember being conscious of any fields beyond the trees.

"Maybe we'll come across some place that's just terrific," Margaret said.

"It's pretty, isn't it?"

"Like a bad painting." Margaret began to hum to herself. Chip leaned against her, but he didn't go to sleep. The trees stopped for a while and then they started again. I remember that I kept wondering what it would be like to hear a love song when you were an old man. I wondered if it would be like anything. I started to ask Margaret about it, and then I didn't.

It was probably about three o'clock when we reached the park. My wristwatch had stopped, and I didn't bother to wind it. The time didn't matter.

Margaret sat up suddenly. "What did I tell you? Something terrific."

"You been asleep?"

"No, of course not."

"Damn," Chip said, or something that sounded like it.

The name of the place was Highland Park. We're sure of that. The letters were written over the entrance in electric bulbs. We noticed when we left that one of the bulbs in the G had burned out. I swung the car under the bulbs that spelled HIGHLAND PARK. A man at the gate came out and smiled at us.

"Thirty cents. A dime for each rider and a dime for the car." The man spoke slowly as if he had all of the time in the world.

"But there are three of us." I nodded at Chip. He sat up and blinked his eyes. The side of his face was red and there was perspiration around the line of his hair.

"You got a fine boy," the man said. "No charge for him."

"But we want to pay for him," Margaret said. "It's his birthday."

"No charge." The man gave me my change, a Franklin half dollar and two dimes. I made the car follow some arrows to the parking place.

"It's funny. I wanted to pay for him too," I said.

"We will." Margaret patted her handkerchief around Chip's forehead and neck. "Chip will be a big boy and someday . . ." She wasn't thinking about what she was saying because she stopped and said, "Look, Chip, a swimming pool. A wonderful big swimming pool."

"What do you think of that, Chip?"

"I wonder why nobody's ever told us about this place." Right away Margaret began taking off Chip's clothes.

There wasn't any charge for Chip again, even though we explained about its being his birthday. I told Margaret I'd take him with me, since I dressed faster than she did. Chip wore a pair of training pants. He looked pretty proud of himself. I put him in the wire basket which the desk man had given me. Chip's eyes were big and he said, "Water." Then he said something that sounded like "Oogle," and I said it back to him. We had quite a conversation while I got into the rented trunks.

"Bye," Chip said, and I said, "Bye."

"You're crazy about that kid, aren't you?" A man spoke behind me. I turned around quickly because I had thought we were the only people in the dressing room. The man wore white swimming trunks and his skin was very brown.

"He's a good guy," I told the man. "This is his birthday."

"You can tell that all right," the man said.

I slipped the elastic identification bracelet around my ankle, and took Chip out of the basket. "Is the water good?"

"The water's fine." The man had disappeared by the time I turned to take my clothes back to the desk. I could hear his feet splash through the antiseptic trough outside the dressing room.

The concrete floor was slick. I slipped once. I held to Chip. He laughed as if we had a joke.

Margaret was waiting for us. "Now who dresses fast?" She stood at the edge of the sand which led to the pool. She pulled at the sides of a white bathing cap, and she ran ahead of us over the sand. I was surprised at how much sand they had around the pool. It was like a regular beach. Margaret looked wonderful in the rented bathing suit. It was the color of the yellow sand.

Chip grunted and held to my neck. My shoulder was sunburned from working in the yard and he hurt like the devil. I told him so.

"You know what the last one in is," Margaret shouted. "Hurry!" She beat the water with her hands.

Chip liked the pool right from the first. We stayed in the shallow end the whole time. I don't remember anybody around us, but Margaret says there were some children and a few parents. The place was big though. I told Margaret I ought to go back to the car and get the new ball, but she said there wasn't any need. We took turns swinging Chip through the water.

After a while a wind came up from somewhere. Chip began to shiver a little and we decided it was time to go in. Chip didn't want to get out of the water. He cried and kicked at me, and Margaret kept saying, "Look here, look here, is that our Chip?"

It was almost cold in the dressing room. There wasn't anybody at the desk so I reached over the counter and got the wire basket. A couple of towels with HIGHLAND PARK written on them lay on top of our clothes. The G was blurred. I dried Chip as well as I could. "Look here, look here," I kept saying. I slapped my foot down against the floor and splashed water. The floor was covered with water now. I wondered at the time if the wind had driven the water out of the pool. Chip sniffed and chewed at his upper lip.

But when we met Margaret we forgot about the wind. We took our picnic basket to a table which was shaded by a red and white umbrella. Chip sat in Margaret's lap. "What shall we have for the birthday boy?" Margaret asked. Chip was frowning and then he began to laugh. He said, "Water," and he patted Margaret's arm with his hand.

I ordered a couple of beers and Margaret asked the waiter if it would be too much trouble to fix the juice of two oranges, no water, and to sterilize the glass. The waiter said it wouldn't be any trouble at all. Generally, when we had Chip out we looked around to see who was watching—that's the way we judged people: if they smiled at Chip they were good characters. But we didn't look at anybody that afternoon in Highland Park. The table was an island. We talked about things which we both knew well. I didn't pay for the orange juice—that came to me only yesterday. I had looked at the bill that afternoon too. I had noticed that it was written in a small backhand, like a woman's writing. I thought at the time that it would be a crazy joke if God turned out to be a woman.

When we finished eating, we walked around a little. Highland Park was big. It seemed to stretch clear to the edge of the land. There was a pavilion for dancing. The orchestra men were already standing at the gate. They wore white suits and dark blue ties. There was even a theater with "Air Cooled" on the marquee in letters that were covered with snow. We couldn't know what time it was, but we knew it was getting late.

"We have time for a ride, though, don't we?" I said.

"Maybe one. Would you like to take a fun ride, Chip?"

Chip rubbed his eyes with the back of his hand. He looked shy. He had just started looking shy that week.

We decided on the ferris wheel. It was big, like everything in Highland Park, but it moved slowly, the way a sleepy mind moves. I didn't even try to pay Chip's fare to the man who stood at the bottom of the wheel. We told Chip to notice the bulbs, no bigger than Christmas tree lights, that outlined the spokes of the wheel. Chip looked at them, but he didn't say anything.

It was a long ride for eleven cents. The man who pressed the stick smiled at us every time we curved down past him. He was a big man, and he reminded me of the fellow in the white trunks at the bathhouse, or the waiter, but I can't remember his face. Margaret thinks that his eyes were dark, but I can't remember his eyes.

Once the wheel stopped when we were at the very top. Chip pushed against the rail which fastened us in. It was light still, but suddenly the bulbs on the wheel blinked on. They were blinding at first. I couldn't see anything but the lights which were threaded through the wheel. After a minute the Park beneath us came back into place. The bulbs were in soft colors and Chip tried to reach for them.

"We have to get home, don't we, I guess?" Margaret said. She spoke loudly, as if she had to shout above the soft light. I nodded to her. "We're going to have to go home," she said to the man as we swung past him.

The man smiled. He took us around another time, and then the wheel stopped and the seat we were in rocked back and forth like a cradle.

"Thank you very much," Margaret said. "Very fine ride."

"Thanks," Chip said, or something that sounded like it.

The man did not speak. We are sure of that.

When we passed the theater two young people were dancing in the foyer to a kind of Negro spiritual with a heavy rhythm background. It seemed strange for them to be dancing to a hymn. Margaret said that it seemed strange to her too.

Chip was sound asleep before we got to the car. I laid him on his mattress. Margaret and I stood and watched him, our arms around each other. He rolled over once and then he settled on his back, gone to the world. His right arm was thrown above his head, and the fingers of his hands were loose.

"Don't you wish you could sleep like that?" I said.

"Don't I?" Margaret said. I didn't know what she meant.

I helped her in the car and closed the door carefully. Then I got in on my side and started the engine and eased out of the parking lot. No one was at the gate. Margaret said that we had forgotten to bring a blanket. "But we didn't forget much, did we?" She was whispering.

"Not much," I said, and we both laughed.

Margaret stood on her knees and covered Chip with one of the diapers from the basket. "Do you mind putting your window up?" she said. "The air's stronger back there."

I put the window up and we started through the cave of trees. I pulled at Margaret's shoulder and she moved over beside me. "Yeah," I said.

"It's not like any day, is it?"

"That's right."

The road curved. Margaret leaned forward. "You'd think we could see the lights from the Park, wouldn't you?"

"Maybe we've come too far."

Once Margaret said, "I hope I remembered to turn off the gas under the water heater," and once I asked her if she wanted a cigarette, and once she read a highway sign aloud, "Slow Cattle Crossing." I don't remember anything else we said until just before the city limit of Carrollton. Margaret spoke so softly that I didn't hear her at first; "I guess nobody could write *Pilgrim's Progress* anymore, could they?"

"Could *he*." Margaret looked up at me. She did not smile. "Sure, sure," I said.

"No, I mean really." Margaret moved away from me. The courthouse was lit up as if it were a funeral parlor or a part of Highland Park.

"There's no point in trying to scare ourselves."

Margaret did not answer.

Beside us was a White Castle hamburger place. Ahead, a street light changed from green to red. A policeman stood on the corner.

I asked, "You want something else to eat?"

"What about Chip?" Margaret placed her hand on the back of the seat to turn around.

"We'll eat in the car." I put on the brakes. Margaret almost lost her balance. "Sorry," I said.

"Why don't you just back up?"

"Isn't there a fireplug?"

"Not much of a one." Margaret was on her knees.

"But there's much of a cop. We'll go around the block." I hummed a tune under my breath. I switched on the dims. The policeman looked at us.

"Chip!" Margaret called.

"Careful, you'll wake him." The light turned to green.

Margaret sucked in her breath. She put her hand on my shoulder. Her hand hurt my shoulder.

"What's the matter with you?" I turned my head. Margaret's face was green in the light. Her eyes were wide and her mouth was opened.

"He's not back here." Margaret spoke softly. The policeman motioned to me. "Chip's not back there."

I reversed the car to the curb beside the fireplug. A sign said, "No Parking Within Ten Feet."

Margaret clicked the light above her head. I put my elbow on the back of the seat, and I leaned on my elbow, and I looked at the mattress. The sheet was rumpled and I could see the outline where Chip's body had been. The plastic ball with the bell inside of it lay in the corner.

I took my left hand and put it on the door handle and pressed down the door handle and the door opened. I stepped down to the ground. I turned around and I pushed back the seat. Chip was not in the car.

The policeman came up to me.

I looked over at Margaret. She lowered her head.

"You havin' some trouble or something?" the policeman said. He was tall and he wore glasses. The right shaft of his glasses was taped with adhesive.

Margaret raised her head. I could see the pulse beating in her throat. "Could you tell us the way to . . . Highland Park?" she asked.

"Highland Park?" The policeman took off his cap. The cap had left a line on his forehead, and above the line were drops of perspiration. "You sure you got the right name?"

"Highland Park," I said.

"There's Melody Park." The policeman nodded. "You take 32 straight out. You can't miss it."

"No, Highland Park," Margaret said. "It's an amusement park. They have a swimming pool, and a theater, and rides."

"There's Melody Park," the policeman said. "But it's not like that. It's a fine place though. They have bands sometimes."

Tears were in Margaret's eyes, but her voice was even. "It's Highland Park we want. HIGHLAND. A bulb is burned out of the G."

"If there was such a place around here, I'd know it, lady. I been born and raised here."

"Well, thank you, then." Margaret pushed back the seat and motioned to me. "We mustn't stay here by that fireplug."

I looked at the policeman for a long time. I couldn't see him very well. I wondered if it were the chlorine in the water that made me not see him very well.

"Melody's a mighty nice place," the policeman said.

Margaret held her hands in her lap. The light from the dashboard showed her hands. She rubbed the nail of her left thumb with the ball of her right thumb.

"God damn." Her words sounded like praying.

But, of course, we couldn't find the road. It was almost daylight when Margaret said, "I guess it doesn't happen to many people . . . this way."

"Margaret?"

"We'd better go home."

She was on her knees. I knew what she was going to reach for. "Please don't. For God's sake, please don't." I didn't mean to shout at her.

She turned around. She hadn't even touched the ball, but the movement of the car made the bell ring.

The Prayer Meeting

Mrs. Bemis had as good sense as anyone in Lexington, Kentucky, but she liked to pretend she was crazy. After her husband, the Reverend Alfred Bemis, died, after she stopped going to church because of her blood pressure, after the days were filled only with her daughter's chattering care, Mrs. Bemis was compelled to create entertainment for herself. She planned her projects carefully, stretching them out to cover as much time as possible. She patched the projects together from scraps of the past, but the present was infinitely more attractive than the past had ever been. Nothing annoyed her more than for her daughter Alphie to start carrying on about "the other days." Alphie was the limit, five feet seven and every inch a fool. It served her right to be named Alphie. Mrs. Bemis had wanted her second child to be a boy. When the doctor announced a girl, Mrs. Bemis had named her Alphie on the spot. She considered Alphie Bemis the ugliest name she had ever heard.

The first daughter, Anne, had run away and married. She died a long time ago, leaving a son whom Mrs. Bemis considered a half-wit. He was twenty-five and still studying to be a church educational director at the Seminary in Louisville. Mrs. Bemis ordered Alphie to call him long-distance and invite him to the prayer meeting. But she talked about the prayer meeting for two months before the telephone call. At first she had considered inviting everybody in Lexington. Finally, though, she decided on Alphie, Alfred II, and Martha Wattlington for the congregation.

Number Two was a very conscientious boy, so of course he promised to take the bus clear down from Louisville the very next night. Mrs. Bemis always referred to young Alfred as Two or Number Two. It seemed to get his goat. Alphie kept saying, "Remember the other days," over the telephone. Mrs. Bemis could not hear Number Two's voice, of course, but she felt sure he was saying, "Oh, yes, Aunt Alphie. Oh, yes, I remember the other days."

Mrs. Bemis telephoned fat Martha Wattlington herself. She made Alphie dial the number, of course. Martha said she'd be glad to come, she'd been meaning to get over all week. It was amazing what an old voice Martha had over the telephone. Mrs. Bemis laughed into the receiver in spite of herself. Martha had lived neighbor in Paducah, and now they were all back in Lexington—what was left of them. Martha had a grandson, ten years old, and you'd never think to look at her that she once wore spit curls. Martha was one of the first women in Paducah to get a bob. Reverend Bemis never said a word against Martha's hair, but he raised the roof when Anne had hers cut. Reverend Bemis always said Martha Wattlington was a true Christian gentlewoman.

"You'll get your grandson to come for you," Mrs. Bemis said sweetly to the telephone. O. C. Wattlington often walked Martha home. "It does my heart good to see that child." O. C. looked more like a rabbit than a boy. It was his teeth that did it. Nobody ever had two bigger front teeth than O. C. Wattlington. Mrs. Bemis told Martha she liked to keep in touch with the youngest generation, and Martha said O. C. would be glad to drop by.

Number Two arrived before Martha. The Bemis men were always early. If Reverend Bemis didn't get to church an hour ahead, he thought he was late. Mrs. Bemis barely had time to put on a funny outfit before the doorbell was ringing. She had meant to drape some toilet paper around her neck like a scarf, but there just wasn't time.

Two leaned way over to kiss Mrs. Bemis and he stood straight to kiss Alphie. Alphie cried a little, naturally, and clung to him, and said, "Baby, baby." The boy finally pulled himself away from the snottering Alphie, and he squared his thin shoulders, and he said, "You're looking mighty well, Grandmother."

"Nice or well?" she asked him. She turned around slowly so he could get the full effect of her regalia. Over the yellowed pongee she had bought in Paducah thirty years ago, she had placed one of Reverend Bemis' collarless shirts, and over that a red blouse of Alphie's.

"Both nice and well," Number Two said.

Mrs. Bemis pirouetted faster. She laughed because she was making the church educational director lie in his teeth. She twirled so swiftly that her pigtails stood almost straight out. Alphie had tried to make her put her hair up, but Mrs. Bemis had insisted on the pigtails with yarn bows. "You really think I look nice?" she gasped over the laughter.

"Oh, yes, very nice," Number Two said in his preacher's voice.

When Martha came, Mrs. Bemis acted as if her own layered costume were normal prayer meeting attire. Martha was decked out like a horse and buggy as usual—gloves and purse and perfume smelling to high heaven. She shook Mrs. Bemis' hand for a long time and said, "How good it is to see you!" Martha always did show her gums when she smiled, but it was worse now that she had false teeth.

Alphie wanted to tell people where to sit, but Mrs. Bemis wouldn't let her. She put Alphie and Martha on the piano bench, and Two across the room in the Morris chair. She herself sat on the arm of Number Two's chair.

"Your granddaddy's back," Mrs. Bemis covered her mouth with her hand so Martha and Alphie would think she was talking about them.

"Oh?" Two said, straightening the crease in his left trousers' leg.

"He's been back from the dead for a week, now." You could tell Number Two almost anything. He looked up at Mrs. Bemis with such trustful cow eyes that Mrs. Bemis had difficulty in keeping her face straight. "I think he's liking me better," she said, which gave her an excuse to laugh.

"That's fine," Two said.

"He doesn't spend so much time with that woman any more down at the hotel. I don't mean Martha Wattlington, I mean the other one, the dancer with bobbed hair." Reverend Bemis had been terribly opposed to dancing. Of all the sins, he considered dancing the worst.

"We were going to have a prayer meeting." Two cleared his throat. "Prayer meeting." He didn't spell out the words, but he gave the impression of spelling.

Mrs. Bemis made her eyes go blank. "By the way, I've been wanting to have a prayer meeting." She spoke loudly.

Alphie jumped to her big feet. "Little Mother has been yearning for a prayer meeting." Alphie had tears in her eyes. Alphie enjoyed nothing more than following company to the front door and crying and saying that Mrs. Bemis had to be handled with kid gloves. "You just can't force my little mother," Alphie always told the departing guests.

"Who?" Mrs. Bemis asked.

"We can have Alfred lead us," Alphie said patiently.

"I don't know anybody else to do it." Mrs. Bemis shook her head. The pigtails on her back swayed. She shook her head harder and the pigtails moved more swiftly. She leaned her head back, and the pigtails waved hilariously.

"Mother," Alphie said. "Little Mother."

Mrs. Bemis pretended to slip from the chair arm. Alphie and Martha and Two were beside her in a flash.

"Thank you, thank you," Mrs. Bemis said, making her body as heavy as possible. She allowed them to place her in the Morris chair before she got up to walk over to the sliding doors which led to the dining room.

"Wait until the prayer meeting is over," Two said. There was a touch of impatience in his voice which caused Mrs. Bemis to smile at him over her shoulder.

"It's been a lovely day," Martha Wattlington said.

"Lovely." Alphie was about to cry. You could tell from her voice that she was about to cry. "And how are all your folks?"

Mrs. Bemis stood listening at the sliding door. "I think your father's back there, Alphie," she said. "I wish you'd tell him to come in for the meeting."

"Oh, Mother," Alphie said, but she went.

Martha Wattlington said, "We certainly did use to have some good times together—all our families."

"We certainly did," Mrs. Bemis said, and Alphie was back. It would have been a good opportunity to discuss adultery, but Alphie didn't give them time.

"He wasn't there," Alphie said.

Mrs. Bemis began to breathe heavily. She bit her lips together. It was a trick which always worked on Alphie.

"He was there, but he said he had a headache."

"That's different." Mrs. Bemis smiled at Alphie who was a great fool. "He's just been subject to headaches for the last few days," she explained to Martha. "I hope it isn't his eyes."

Number Two was looking at his wristwatch, so Mrs. Bemis opened the sliding doors into the dining room and told him to follow her.

"You'd better go," Alphie said. "It's probably something about the prayer meeting."

It was difficult to talk to anybody as half-witted as Two without laughing in his face, but Mrs. Bemis managed very nicely. She told him she had been worried about the singers. Two said they had enough singers. Mrs. Bemis told him that the doctor had sung to her yesterday and then pinched her knee. Two looked scared out of his half-wits, and led her back into the living room.

Naturally Two sat down at the piano. Mrs. Bemis had always thought it unseemly for a man to play the piano, particularly at prayer meeting. It served Two right to be able to play. She made him get up so she could get the three hymn books out of the bench. She insisted on handing out the books, trading them around several times. Alphie looked as if she were about to go crazy. Mrs. Bemis made Alphie and Martha sit on the couch, and then on the radiator. She stuffed Martha's gloves under the cushion of the Morris chair and sat on them.

"I'm afraid you won't be comfortable there," she told Martha and Alphie. "The couch, please."

"Mother. Little Mother," Alphie said, but she and Martha moved.

" 'Dwelling in Beulah Land.' Number Two Three Seven," Mrs. Bemis said. "The first hymn will be 'Dwelling in Beulah Land.' " It was the hymn she disliked most. Next to "The Star-Spangled Banner" she considered it the most impossible song in the English language.

Two's hands were quite large and ugly. He hit the keys as if he were angry at them. Alphie said, "The soft pedal," placing her finger on her lips.

"Everybody sing," Two said.

The singing was a lovely fiasco, of course. Two sang so loudly that you couldn't hear yourself, and Martha held the notes longer than anybody. Mrs. Bemis got the full benefit of both of their dreadful voices. Alphie, of course, never had any voice. She took after her father, and besides she was terribly touched by the occasion. She kept rubbing her eyes with the back of her hand.

"Again," Mrs. Bemis said when they had finished all the verses. "Standing as we sing."

Two struck a chord. "You stand, too, Two," Mrs. Bemis said, and Two stood too. It was hilarious. Mrs. Bemis laughed until she cried.

"Again," she said. "All the verses." Her plans for the service had included only one singing of the song, but it was all too delightful.

"One more verse. This time, humming the chorus."

Mrs. Bemis would have demanded a fourth complete rendition, but she fagged out with laughing and standing up for so long. "Be seated, please," she said.

Martha Wattlington was fagged out, too. She was breathing as heavily as anybody in the room, and she was twelve and a half years younger than Mrs. Bemis.

"Anne is the angriest girl you ever saw," Mrs. Bemis said, folding her hands over her stomach. "She told me she was going to beat her daddy up. She said she was going to whip him within an inch of his life."

"Please, Grandmother," Two said, swinging his legs to the congregation side of the piano bench. Two couldn't bear for Mrs. Bemis to talk about his dead mother; he was very sentimental about motherhood. On Mother's Day he always sent Mrs. Bemis a card full of lace and sugar. He even sent Alphie a card, less lace and less sugar, but a card nevertheless, which showed how Two's mind ran.

"Anne said, 'If I can't beat him up myself, I'll make Two help me.' " Mrs. Bemis nodded at Two's legs. "She was sitting right on that very bench. She said it yesterday A.M. at half-past seven."

Two looked down at his legs, as if he expected to find his mother on the floor. Mrs. Bemis feigned a coughing fit. Alphie was at her side, of course, fanning her with an antimacassar. Alphie never could find a fan when she needed one.

"I'm all right, Alphie," Mrs. Bemis said weakly. "Take your seat."

"Don't you want to lie down and rest a while, Little Mother?" Alphie asked. "We mustn't get too excited and hot. It's bad for us if we get too hot."

"Seated," Mrs. Bemis said, refusing to allow anyone to speak until Alphie was back by Martha Wattlington. Two tried to speak. Three times he said, "Prayer meeting." Finally Mrs. Bemis had to say, "Your mother told me to tell you to keep silent."

And, finally, Alphie sat down.

Mrs. Bemis cleared her throat. "I said, 'Go to it, Daughter Anne. I'm with you.' She said, 'Mother, he'll ruin us all with that dancer down at the hotel.' "

"Mother, Mother, please," Alphie said, the tears starting again.

"Well," Mrs. Bemis smoothed the antimacassar over her knees.

She didn't look straight at Martha Wattlington, but she snatched little glances at her big fat face. Martha looked scared to death, as well she might. Her mouth was open and her eyes were like holes burned in a blanket. "Well, I heard water running in the bathtub."

"Grandmother, we have come for a prayer meeting." Two was standing now. He had pulled a Bible out of his jacket pocket.

"Please, Two." Mrs. Bemis made her voice sweet and patient. "Please, do not be sacrilegious."

Two sat down all right.

"As I was saying, there was your grandfather and the dancer in the bathtub, splashing and singing for all they were worth. I was heart-sick. I told Anne not to look. I said, 'Daddy, get out of that tub.' "

"You dreamed it, Mother. You dreamed it." Alphie leaned her head against the back of the couch. At least she didn't stand up, which proved she was smarter than Two.

"They were just splashing away. It was the worst sight I ever saw."

"You know you dreamed it," Alphie said. "The bathtub isn't big enough for two people."

"The dancer is smaller than your father," Mrs. Bemis said patiently.

Alphie didn't answer. She just shook her head against the back of the couch.

"Are you denying that the dancer is smaller?" Mrs. Bemis asked sharply.

"I'm not denying it." Alphie was sometimes difficult to handle, even as a child.

"Excuse me." Mrs. Bemis smiled apologetically first at Martha, then at Two. "Alphie, repeat after me: 'The dancer is smaller than my father.' "

"The dancer is smaller than my father," Alphie said.

Two was up again. He was turning the pages of his Bible. Fortunately, he was all thumbs and the pages stuck together and he couldn't find what he was looking for.

Mrs. Bemis stood, too. "How have you been feeling, Martha?"

"Very well very well very well," Martha said all in a breath. She was holding tight to the arm of the couch. "I've been very well, Mrs. Bemis."

"Do you remember when we lived in Paducah and you had your hair cut?" Mrs. Bemis smiled and nodded at Martha Wattlington.

"Indeed I do, Mrs. Bemis." Martha laughed so loudly that she evidently scared herself. She let go of the couch arm, and she sat very straight.

"We will have silent prayer." Mrs. Bemis seated herself and spread the drapery of Reverend Bemis's shirttails neatly over her knees. "We will dedicate this meeting to my husband, Reverend Alfred Bemis, who has a headache in the back bedroom."

The group was remarkably cooperative. Once Alphie whispered something to Martha and Martha answered; and twice Two said, "Amen." But you couldn't call them disorderly. Mrs. Bemis said, "Please," squeezing her eyelids so tightly that she saw rainbows. "Please, all of you."

The house was very quiet. If there had been a splashing in the bathtub, they could have heard it. But Mrs. Bemis didn't allow herself to think of the bathtub story; she absolutely refused to laugh during the silent prayer period. Too, it was pleasant to watch the rainbows burst in the darkness of the quiet living room. She probably would have lost track of time if Martha Wattlington's grandson hadn't rung the doorbell.

"Amen," Mrs. Bemis said, and Alphie was out in the foyer in a flash. Alphie loved to answer the door.

"I came for my grandmother," O. C. Wattlington said in his squeaking voice.

Alphie was all over herself being gracious. "Come right in, come right in, O. C." Alphie had her arm around the boy's shoulders. Alphie just couldn't keep her hands off people.

"Shake hands with Mrs. Bemis," Martha said.

In spite of herself, Mrs. Bemis said, "Would you like a carrot, O. C.?"

Alphie said, "Why, Mother."

O. C. said, "No thank you, mam."

"Could you sing me a little song?" Mrs. Bemis refused to let go of the boy's hand. He was a patient, dull child, and after two or three yanks he let his hand stay in hers.

"Can you sing for Mrs. Bemis?" Martha began to gather herself together. She was looking for the gloves, of course.

"We are having a prayer meeting," Mrs. Bemis said. "Do you know any appropriate prayer meeting songs?"

"I don't think so," O. C. said through his rabbit teeth. He couldn't look you in the eye, and he had an outlandish cowlick. Mrs. Bemis felt sure he was the funniest child she had ever seen, unless it was Two at the same age, but she kept her face straight.

"Your grandmother is a very religious gentlewoman," Mrs. Bemis said. "Are you sure you don't have a single, solitary, prayer meeting song?"

"I don't think so." O. C. pulled at his hand a little, but only a little.

"The prayer meeting is dismissed, then," Mrs. Bemis said. "Did you lose something, Martha?"

"Just gloves," Martha said, wallowing around on the couch. "It doesn't matter. It's been awfully nice seeing you." But Martha still looked for the gloves. She was a great one for her possessions.

"What kinds of songs do you know?" Mrs. Bemis spoke each word slowly. O. C.'s face was getting white under his freckles.

"He knows 'Davy Crockett.' " Martha was exasperated. Her face was red. White O. C. and red Martha made an interesting combination for anybody's eyes.

Mrs. Bemis let go of O. C.'s hand for a moment. She clapped her own hands together, although there was really no need to get the group any quieter. They were as quiet as death already. "We will all stand while Master O. C. Wattlington favors us with 'Davy Crockett.' "

Two had turned around to the keyboard. Two never missed a chance to show off.

"He will sing *a cappella*," Mrs. Bemis said sternly.

"It is very difficult to sing unaccompanied"—Two's Adam's apple worked in his thin throat—"unaccompanied under these conditions."

Mrs. Bemis closed her eyes. "Your mother came from the dead and told me to ask you never to play the piano again."

It was a splendid thing to say. The words just came to Mrs. Bemis. She had planned almost every other detail of the evening, but the piano business was a lovely bolt from the blue. Two got to his feet as if he were a very old man. Mrs. Bemis liked to hope it would be some time before he returned to his music.

"As soon as your grandmother stands, you may proceed, O. C.," Mrs. Bemis said softly.

"You may proceed."

O. C.'s thin little voice moved painfully from one note to another. His hand worked convulsively in Mrs. Bemis' tight grasp. Once he forgot the words, and Martha, her head bowed, supplied, "His politickin' done." It was a very long song, and hideously rendered.

"Thank you, O. C. Thank you very much," Mrs. Bemis said. "And now, before you release my frail hand, I want you to promise to remember—as long as you live I want you to remember . . ."

"It's late. He has school tomorrow," Martha Wattlington said, as if she knew what Mrs. Bemis was going to say. She couldn't have known, of course, but she moved quickly, for her bulk, across the room, and she stood breathing heavily beside her rabbit of a grandson.

"Remember that your grandmother took a bath with my husband," Mrs. Bemis said sweetly. "They splashed together."

"Grandmother!" Two shouted.

"She doesn't know what she's saying," Alphie sobbed.

"Oh Mrs. Bemis." Martha's voice was a long wail.

The Rabbit didn't say anything.

Mrs. Bemis sank carefully to the floor. It was really the best place to end the meeting, here, now, in the lovely present. She had planned to close with a solo dance. But she had hexed Two's piano playing, and it was foolish to dance without music. Anyhow, she had already overexerted herself. Her blood pressure was up again. She could tell when it was up.

She did not bat an eyelash as they carried her to the back bedroom. Two was already promising Alphie he would stand by her. Two had the Bemis loyalty. Mrs. Bemis would be gravely ill for at least several weeks, and Two would get terribly behind with his work at the Seminary—all for the sake of "the other days." Martha Wattlington would send in custard and broth until it was running out of their ears. And Alphie . . . oh, that funny, stupid Alphie.

They placed her carefully on the bed. Mrs. Bemis thought about pretending that Reverend Bemis lay on the bed beside her. But she didn't. Instead, she went straight to sleep.

The Cardboard Screen

It had been a mistake to invite them, but at the moment it had seemed as natural as the breeze which pulled at the soft ribbons of the heaped flowers. Della had not closed her eyes during the benediction; she looked steadily at the yellow glads she and Charlie had sent. One streamer of the white ribbon flipped itself over at the Amen. She turned; she lifted her feet high so that she would not step on any graves, even the old ones, and moved to each of the girls. "We'll sew tomorrow," Della said. "As usual." Her face felt drawn from not crying, as if she were a child who had left soap to dry on her skin. Her mother had always said, "Be sure and dry your face, Della." And all of their mothers had told them not to step on the graves. Other Junes they had walked through the cemetery with their mothers, taking a shortcut to the park.

Betty Kay bobbed her head; her eyes were squeezed tight; she pressed her gloved hand hard against her mouth. Winifred's eyes swam, almost invisible in her tears, but she smiled down at Della. "We'll sew tomorrow as usual." Three times Della said the words. Lillian did not cry, but her face looked as old as her mother's face beside her. Of course the woman who wore Lillian's suit was Lillian. Della was conscious of the woof and warp of the linen. She thought, as briefly as the ribbon's flip, that she should pat Lillian's arm. Instead, she went to find Charlie, her own invitation still in her ears. "We'll sew tomorrow, Della," she said to herself. None of the girls had answered her.

In the car Charlie said, "It was a nice service."

"What are we going to do, Charlie?" she asked before she thought of what to say.

She could not look at his face. His shoe pressed against the gas pedal, then relaxed. He was wearing the black shoes she had bought for him a long time ago. They needed polishing. "But I got black shoes," Charlie said. "They're so old, the other ones. You need black shoes when you dress up," Della said. Dust lay on the shoes. It was dust from Charlie's closet. The cemetery was green.

"Della, look at me," the man in the old black shoes said. "I love you, Della."

The car trembled. If she closed her eyes perhaps she could know which person in Charlie's body was saying, "I love you, Della, you know that." There was Charlie who sold Fords, and Charlie Somebody on the School Board, and somebody else who lived on Parkview with his wife and two sons, but the boys were away at camp. There was Charlie who had had an affair.

"Look at me, Della, honey."

"I just don't want to cry." Charlie's wife could not close her eyes. As sudden as the turn of a ribbon or Amen she could not close her eyes.

"Please."

His hand moved across the seat toward her. The hand was big and freckled; fine red hair covered it. She nodded at three blurred faces in a black car which pulled past them over the gravel drive. The hand disappeared.

He said, "Josephine didn't have anything to do with us. Listen to me. I'm trying to talk to you."

"I said we wouldn't mention her again, not ever again," she said aloud, or to herself. "We weren't going to mention her."

"She was a sick woman, in her mind, too. I told you I was sorry. I try to tell you. You don't give me a chance."

Charlie spoke the words easily. He could have been addressing his employees. She thought of saying, "Maybe you just know the easy words."

"It's why she drank so much. And slept around. A lot of men

could tell you. I'm not saying it was right. I'm just trying to tell you." His voice was a straight line. "It didn't mean anything. I've been trying to tell you."

She was calm. It was the car that trembled, waiting to pull into the string of traffic, which only an hour ago had been a funeral procession. "The way's clear," she said. "You can get in line now." She said, "I don't mean that. I don't mean anything. Just don't talk to me."

She could have said, "We have each other." That would have been something to say. Perhaps, if she had not invited the girls, she would have said, the way people in real life were always saying, "We have each other." She could have cried, and Charlie could have comforted her in the empty house. They could have held each other in the empty house. She could remember Charlie's face above her, saying, "I love you, I love you."

"We had a letter from Tim," she said. "They like camp. Bobby finally passed his swimming test. You can read it."

"Later," Charlie said.

They were in the driveway beside a house on Parkview Road. She held her gloved hand on the car door. She said, "You're not coming in." She was not sure if she spoke a question or a statement.

"Later, later," Charlie said. The tires of his car turned slowly, and then the driveway held only the blotched shade of the maple tree they had planted a long time ago.

She had not cried. Even after the moon came up white and round she had not cried. She undressed and lay at the foot of the bed, looking at the moon. Several times the telephone rang. It's Winifred. It's Lillian. It's Betty Kay. It's Charlie, even, calling, she told herself, but she did not move from the bed.

Once upon a time there was a time before Charlie. He hadn't even known about Madison, Kentucky, where kites sailed over the park. When the five girls were growing up he hadn't ever been out of Tennessee. It was strange to think about. They played hide-and-seek. They took turns giving slumber parties. They went to dances. Josephine was first. Josephine had the first permanent, and the first two-piece bathing suit, and the first car of her own. She was married first. But they had followed quickly. Josephine was divorced first. She was the only one to be divorced. Josephine knew about death first, too. Death was a word like hide-and-seek. It was something to remember, like time.

But Della did not look at her watch when Charlie finally came home. It was late. She hurried her body around to lie straight in the bed, the way bodies were supposed to lie in bed. She covered herself carefully with the sheet. She breathed carefully, like a sleeping body. Charlie tiptoed to his closet to get his pajamas. He stood by the bed. He breathed harshly. And after a while he went away to sleep in another bed in the cool dark house; and after a while she slept, the night heavy against her eyelids. All of them slept alone. When she awoke Charlie had left the house again; there was no proof he had stood beside her on the night of Josephine's funeral.

It was ten o'clock. She watched her own hand with the kitchen scissors whose broken prongs bit into the chicken. She had already taken the transparent pies from the oven. When Mamma was alive she always said transparent pies were the nicest compliment you could pay your guests. And now Mamma had passed away. All of their mothers had passed away. And their fathers, too. Except Lillian's mother. Lillian's mother had looked very young at Josephine's funeral.

"Josephine Nye Martin Foster is dead," Della said aloud.

She called all of Josephine's names. Josephine no longer pretended to sleep under the flowers. Josephine Nye Martin Foster was and isn't.

Della leaned heavily against the sink. She had wished herself dead. For five months she had almost wished herself dead. *Death* was a real word, like *scissors* or *salad.* She could not think of anything to wish.

On four white Spode plates she arranged lettuce; it expanded, and she heard the movement of the lettuce, like breath. She reached her hand toward the table. In a little while Winifred and Betty Kay and Lillian, grown women, almost-forty-year-old women, would stand on the front porch, breathing against the screen. "Anybody home?" Winifred would call as she had been calling for all of their lives; with their needles and their fabrics they would enter the house; their faces loomed as large as billboards. Winifred's face said to itself: "Della is having a funeral party." No, honestly no, it's not a celebration. I didn't want Josephine to die of a heart attack. I don't want anybody to die of anything. "Really, really, no."

She would telephone them. She would say, "Don't come. Don't come at all. Really."

Or they weren't planning to come. "We'll sew tomorrow," Della Norris said. Not one of them had answered. They had not heard her invitation. And, anyhow, at the cemetery she wasn't even thinking about Josephine and Charlie. Before God, she was only remembering that today was their sewing day. For over a year they had sewed together on the third Tuesday of every month, ever since Josephine moved back from Louisville, before God.

It was snowing the day Winifred came to tell her about Charlie and Josephine. Winifred sat large in the wing chair, filling the room. Her pale eyes were kind. "Della, sweet, you mustn't brood. Nobody else knows. I'll never tell a soul. It's our secret. But if I were in your position . . ." Della studied the fire in the fireplace as if it were a painting in a frame. In the presence of the painting it was difficult to hear Winifred's voice, or to think about Charlie, or Josephine, or the fire itself. Once old Doctor Ed told Della that her appendix had burst. "If I were in your place, I'd want to know," Winifred said. Her square face was kind. Her heavy body leaned forward in the chair; her hands with their unpainted nails moved toward Della.

"What would you do?" Della whispered. "What does anybody do?"

"It's simple," Winifred said. "It's very simple."

It was simple to pour one's mind into the square efficient box of Winifred's mind. Even afterwards when she spoke to Charlie, it was simple. In Winifred's mind Della said, "I thought it was only fair for you to know I know." She said, "Charles, when faith is gone, there isn't anything else." She was not ashamed of Winifred's voice.

"Della, baby, I love you, you know that," he answered in one of his voices, but she did not bother to try to identify which Charles spoke to her. "I don't know how it happened. I don't know."

"We will not discuss it any more," she said, holding Winifred's mind carefully, bearing Charlie for the sake of the boys, moving through the rest of winter, through five sewing days, past spring, into summer, softly so that she would not spill Winifred's mind. "Courage," Winifred said in their little talks. "That's my Della. You're keeping your chin up."

But Josephine was dead.

Della bit at the knuckles of her hand. "Did you hear? In the cemetery Della Norris lost Winifred's mind? It was like a joke. If she had been alone in the house she could have laughed until she cried tears as salty as the blood on her hand. "She lost Winifred's mind, and she didn't miss it until the next day. She didn't actually miss it until she was getting ready for the funeral party." But she could not laugh because she was not alone in the house. Some place, back in time, she stood and watched herself against the sink. "You're not going to be sick," she said. "You can surely borrow another mind for the day."

"It's all right," somebody told her in the hospital—Mother, or old Doctor Ed, or somebody. "You're going to feel fine when you wake up." She was thirteen. It was almost her thirteenth birthday. But she had not felt wonderful. "I feel wonderful," she said, and somebody pressed a cold enamel basin against her. And now Della Norris had lost Winifred's mind.

If Lillian, or Betty Kay had told her about Charlie and Josephine, she would probably have acted as they expected her to act. But it was Winifred who said, "I think you ought to know. Josephine confessed to me herself." There was nothing in time to compare with, neither sickness nor death. "She confessed quite freely," Winifred said. "I made her confess."

Della Norris lost Winifred's mind. Sweet, adaptable Della lost everybody's mind. Have you heard? Have you heard?

Winifred had to call three times. "Anybody home? Anybody home? Anybody home?"

"I'm just going to steal your cleaning lady, everything looks so nice." Betty Kay pirouetted in the center of the living room, as graceful and slim as she had been in high school. The yellow folds of her skirt moved softly. "Your house always just sparkles."

"God, it's hot outside." Lillian tossed her sewing basket onto the gray couch. "I don't know why we don't get air conditioning. I could kill Ransom over things like air conditioning."

"It's sweet of you to have us." Winifred touched her lips to Della's hair. "It's so sweet, Della."

They moved as if they followed grooves in the carpet: Betty Kay to the mantel to place her purse, to pat her soft dark hair; Lillian to the couch where she sprawled, kicking off her sandals; Winifred to the wing chair by the piano; Betty Kay gliding on her high heels to swoop onto the ottoman, turning her head to smile at Della; Lillian reaching for a pillow to place behind her head; Winifred's large hands already threading a needle.

"My feet hurt," Lillian said. "It makes them hurt worse to see you in those heels."

"Silly," Betty Kay giggled, turning, and turning again. "Della, we're late because they had to wait on me. Everything was in such a mess this morning. Al couldn't find his car keys, and then Kay insisted on . . ."

"I had a fight with little Ransom before breakfast," Lillian said. "He won't flush the commode. Sometimes I could kill that boy."

"You don't mean that, Lillian." Winifred's needle had already begun to outline a pink flower on a white pique collar.

"It's easy for you to shake your head," Lillian said to the ceiling. "Your girls are exactly like you, sweetness and light, and a place for everything. But that Ransom . . ."

"You're not being fair." Betty Kay pushed out her lips. "Ransom is just darling. Why, yesterday Kay was saying . . ."

"If you'll excuse me," Della said. She had planned the words. "If you'll excuse me."

"Sit down and relax," Lillian said.

"Della, you're white as a sheet. Are you feeling bad, Della?" Winifred's embroidery frame hung in the air, as if it would fly to the table, freeing Winifred to push herself up to her feet, to stand in front of Della Norris, encouraging her to tell about Charlie and Josephine.

"No, don't. Don't. I'm fine."

"You're tired. You've gone to trouble."

"How did you hurt your hand?" Lillian asked.

"Oh my goodness," Betty Kay said. In her lap lay a red felt stocking, half covered with green felt trees and silver sequins.

"At the sink," Della said, but Lillian was not listening.

"Oh that Ransom," Lillian said.

"Please, I'm fine." Della lowered herself to the leather chair by the dining room door. She leaned her head against the back of the chair. In the cool room the leather was warm against her neck.

"Did you say that stocking was for next year, or the year after?" Lillian said. "You make me sick being so far ahead."

"It's a beautiful stocking," Winifred's voice said. "You all make such pretty things."

"You don't consider hemming a tea towel as fancy work, do you? Or darning socks?" Lillian swung her legs around to the floor. Her legs were fat and flabby. "Oh God. Goddamn it."

"Lillian, dear. Please!" Winifred placed her needle in the center of a pink leaf. "There is no need to be profane. We mustn't let ourselves get upset. We're all together, all of us. We're not taking sides."

"Josephine helped me cut out this stocking." Betty Kay's eyes were closed. Tears seeped through her long dark lashes. She bit her lips until she looked like a toothless old woman. "Poor Joesphine."

"Oh God, I was afraid it would be this way," Lillian said.

Winifred was across the room. She inched her large body on to the edge of the ottoman; she put her arms around Betty Kay. "There, there, there, there, now."

"But Josephine of all people. She was so alive. And generous. She was so generous, whatever her little faults."

"Ever so generous. But Betty Kay, honey, listen to me." Winifred might have been speaking to one of her daughters. "This is a hard time for all of us. We have to be realistic. We have a lot to be thankful for."

Betty Kay's little dark eyes darted back and forth in her head. "She gave me this pin. I admired it one day, and she said, 'Here, take it.' You remember. She said, 'Here, take it.' "

"She was generous." Winifred's voice was like salve. "It's hard, just the four of us now, meeting to sew, and remembering." Winifred was gray salve.

"I almost wish she hadn't started us on these sewing days." The ends of the silk tie moved under the pin at Betty Kay's neck.

"It was crazy. And just because our mothers sewed." Lillian's voice was harsh. "I told Josephine it was crazy. She just laughed."

"Yes," Della said, but she could not remember her mother's face.

"I think it's been wonderful," Betty Kay said.

"We all thought our mothers were terribly secure in this crazy town. My mother's always telling me how secure they were."

"Josephine was a leader," Winifred said.

"Except having children," Betty Kay said. "It was the only thing she wasn't first in. Do you think she minded a lot?"

"Josephine was a strange one. She ran deep," Winifred said.

"Yes, yes," Della said. "Yes." She felt sly. She was proud of herself. For five months they had sewed together, and Josephine had never guessed she knew. And Lillian didn't know. And Betty Kay didn't know.

Winifred's pale eyes were looking at Della.

"Yes," Della said. And even Winifred didn't know that Della's mind had no words to think. And Della Norris could get through the funeral party all right. She could run the tape recorder and the camera. If she were careful, and she was careful, oh, marvelously careful, if she were careful, she could get all the pictures straight and in order. She could say, "Yes, yes."

She could follow Lillian's eyes. A film of dust lay quietly on the cross bar of the piano bench.

Winifred, Betty Kay, Winifred, Lillian, Betty Kay. The sounds of their voices came slowly. Betty Kay, Winifred. Sometimes the sound almost disappeared, but there were the quick dark turns of Betty Kay's head, the rocking motion of Winifred's body, yes, yes, Lillian's hands clutching each other as they remembered Josephine.

"Our mothers were ladies, weren't they?"

"Oh, God, yes they were Kentucky ladies."

"Now, Lillian."

Their mothers and their grandmothers, poised as cameos or Godey's ladies, sat in the parlor of the house which once stood on this very lot. In the kitchen a maid helped the cook cut up chicken for the salad. The transparent pies waited in the great oven. Outside the girls played together. In a little while they would eat from real china, using linen napkins, in the playhouse which once stood under the willows. The maid—whatever was her name?—brought the food in two wicker hampers. "Now, you all be nice," she said. "Now, be nice ladies."

But Josephine was not at the table.

Betty Kay's head lay against Winifred's lavender shoulder. Winifred said, "There must be a special heaven for poor tortured souls like Josephine." Betty Kay said, "She was so alive. I don't understand." Winifred said, "Some things we aren't supposed to understand. It's God's will, Betty Kay."

Lillian said, "Oh, hell, you both make me sick. She's dead. That's all anybody knows."

"Lillian."

"Josephine would be getting a big laugh out of this."

Betty Kay was standing. "You hear me, Lillian. You're not to talk that way." Betty Kay was steadying herself against Winifred. "You and Josephine—both of you—you were always making fun of religion. And I let you do it because you were my friends. But now . . . now, you're not to talk that way. You hear me?"

Josephine lay in Charlie's arms, smiling at Charlie, smoothing her hands over his body.

Lillian's weeping, close to laughter, whirred in the room. "Don't shout at me. I'm not making fun."

"Of course you're not," Winifred cried.

"Of course not," the recorder said.

Betty Kay and Winifred were on the couch. The girls fluttered together, almost like flames.

Once upon a time Della had a playhouse. In the playhouse was a grate. On a cardboard screen in front of the grate Della drew a picture of a fire. She colored the fire with yellow and orange and red crayons. The flames embraced each other and parted and embraced again.

"I'm scared, I guess, and I'm too old to be scared." It was Lillian. "I oughtn't to be scared."

"We're not so old, honey." It was Betty Kay.

"I'm scared of dying, I guess. Oh God."

"God's in his heaven." It was Betty Kay again.

"We love each other very much. All this . . ." Winifred said to the air. "All this has brought us closer together. We mustn't be upset."

The machines moved very quickly. "We understand, Lillian." Betty Kay's face was as wet as if she had come from the pond beyond the willows. But there wasn't any pond now. Houses stood on the pond. Children they didn't know played in the square yards of the new houses. "I loved Josephine." Mascara streaked Betty Kay's face. They had not worn lipstick when the pond stood. "I'd have done anything in the world for Josephine, you all know that. She loved me, too. But Josephine liked to be shocking. She always acted, I don't know, different."

They had forgotten her, the three of them, the four of them.

"She wasn't really one of us," Winifred said. "Not even when we were in grade school. She was different."

"But we made fun of things together," Lillian said.

"But Josephine did it most. That's right, isn't it, Winifred?"

Winifred nodded. She took her hand from Lillian's to pull at her own shoulder strap.

In the playhouse Della allowed herself to hide behind the screen of the fire only once a game. "Bushel of wheat, bushel of rye," Winifred called, or Lillian, or Betty Kay. Della crouched behind the fire. She was breathing so hard she tried to hold her breath. "Bushel of wheat, bushel of clover, all aren't hid, can't hide over." But none of them had found her hiding place. "Wherever were you?" they asked. "Della's a funny," Josephine said. "Ally ally out's in free," they called while Della hid in one of their minds.

"I don't mean to be disloyal," Lillian said. "We're not nice people. We're awful people."

"Yes," Della said, afraid for a moment that Lillian had discovered her.

"We're not disloyal. Nobody's being disloyal." The volume on Winifred's voice was high. "Life has to go on."

"It's important to try to be honest," Betty Kay said.

"What's honest, oh my God?" Lillian was crying again. Her shoulders shook. Her voice had not changed really, not in all the years.

"Oh, Lillian, honey, Josephine would want us to be brave," Betty Kay said. "Whatever else, she was gallant and brave."

Once Della giggled when Josephine stood in the doorway of the playhouse. "I hear you, I hear you," Josephine said. "You're some place around and I know it. Don't jump and scare me though. Promise you won't scare me, Della."

She had not come out. She did not mean to come out. The game wasn't over.

Winifred was pushing her into the circle when it wasn't her turn. "*O U T* spells *OUT*." King's X, King's X a minute.

"It's so true." Winifred's picture was moving too fast. "Della's the brave one. Della has the bravery for all of us. Come over here,

Della." Winifred patted the arm of the sofa. "We're all together. And you're so good to have us here, just like always, as if nothing had happened."

"It's the way Josephine would want it," Betty Kay said.

They were all three looking at her. They waited for her. Before it had been Betty Kay and Winifred; and Lillian and Josephine; and Della could belong to either side. "Choose. Choose a side," they said. "Whose side you going to be on?"

"No, really. Don't look at me."

"Della, sweet."

"No, really." She held to the chair arms. "I didn't think anything." She spoke slowly, hoping they could hear her from far across the room.

"I've always said Della kept us together. You've always been the sweetest, and the kindest. I've always said that, haven't I?" Winifred asked the others.

"Josephine loved you too," Betty Kay said. "I think you've just been wonderful, what with Charlie . . ."

"Betty Kay," Winifred whispered, but the sound carried.

"Oh you fools," Lillian said, closing her eyes.

"What I mean . . ." Betty Kay put her palms to her cheeks. Her hands moved over her face until they covered her mouth. Her hands dropped to her lap, like papers falling. "I didn't mean anything. I didn't mean anything, Della."

Winifred organized the games. Winifred decided whether they would play dolls or hide-and-seek. Winifred said, "Josephine grabbed at life, anybody's life." The age lines were deep around Winifred's mouth and eyes. "These sewing days were good. We could keep an eye on Josephine." Winifred decided whether they should play Hearts or Truth.

"You told them, didn't you?" Della said quietly. "You told them about Josephine . . ." She was not angry. "And Charlie."

"She was a menace." The lines grew even deeper. "She was a menace all our lives."

"We loved her, of course," Betty Kay said.

"But we're loyal to you, Della. And we love our husbands and children. You understand that."

Lillian's eyes had found the dust under the piano bench again.

The tape had run out. There wasn't any more film in the camera. Della had to clear her throat before she spoke into the quiet room where the other three women sat.

Perhaps she spoke in Josephine's voice, but she did not mind. "I loved Charlie," she said, wondering if her mind were Josephine's. "I love Charlie."

They were quiet again before Betty Kay said, "You're so wonderful, Della."

Winifred said. And Lillian said. And Betty Kay said. And Winifred said.

They spoke their words as their mothers had spoken, finishing out the morning. But they were not their mothers. Summer lay around them. A mind, or a word like faith, hung over Della, like a kite, tugging at her hands.

And Winifred said, and Betty Kay said, and Lillian said.

Della said, "It's ever so late. You must be starved."

Lillian said, "I am. I didn't have any breakfast."

Winifred said, "Nobody cooks like Della."

Betty Kay said, "I know we're going to have transparent pie."

The Penitent

For three days and nights before his fall lecture tour, Ralph Clark was consumed with somebody named Anabel Forsythe. Otherwise he would have checked the map instead of leaving the arrangements to the Consolidated Artists Bureau, a couple of old ladies who sat in an office on East Thirty-third Street with two desks and two telephones and no sense of geography. If he had known how difficult it was for a lecturer to get in and out of St. Zachary's College, he would not have allowed the engagement. But his magazine article, "I Go to College Again," was benefited by his comments on Catholic Education in America. A couple of Catholic columnists tried to raise hell over one sentence. "St. Zachary's social freedom perhaps exceeds its intellectual freedom," Ralph wrote innocently enough. "They drink but they do not read *A Portrait of the Artist as a Young Man*." The magazine editors, a bunch of converts, got terribly excited over the columnists. Fortunately, Father Dominic wrote a charming letter of tribute concerning "the intellectual stimulation of Mr. Clark's visit." Everything worked out, and the publicity hadn't hurt anybody. But, honestly, Ralph had not meant to criticize the good fathers. They were fine. They had turned out fine.

The night before he left town he had engaged in an extravagantly varied and satisfactory lovemaking with Miss Anabel Forsythe. She was a reference librarian who had come to Columbia from Earlton, Kentucky, and fallen madly in love with New York. "I'm absolutely crazy about New York," she kept saying rather drunkenly in her apartment after dinner. They were sitting on her starkly modern couch which she was also crazy about. One of her hands curled itself in Ralph's heavy hair. He said, "New York is an enchanted city," while moving his right hand slowly over Miss Forsythe's back. "I'm just crazy about it," she said.

He had avoided discussing age with Anabel, although he was particularly interested in people's ages. He was forty-one himself, and he regularly admitted it. The Woman's Club ladies said, "But you're fooling, Mr. Clark." Obviously Anabel had left Kentucky longer ago than she would have admitted. She knew the lyrics to an incredible number of popular songs from the thirties. But she was charming. Her hair was softly bright; her skin, unbelievably lovely. "Am I a fitting companion for Ralph Clark, The Modern Renaissance Man?" she asked, bringing her face close. In their brochures the old ladies always referred to him as The Modern Renaissance Man because of the breadth of his interests. Anabel took the title seriously; she was not making fun. "You are unbelievable, too," she said. "And I'm practically a virgin," she said. "That's nice, too, isn't it, Renaissance Man?"

"Very very nice," he said against her breast.

"Renaissance," she said.

That was when he had told her he was going to dedicate the new book to her. It was a cut and paste collection of essays about creativity which would be out in time for Christmas. He had written a long introduction, and the illustrations were magnificent. Anabel was delighted. She said, "I'm so glad to get out of the Acknowledgments."

"We have *made* love," he told Anabel. It was Muriel's sentence. He had not thought of Muriel for a long time. He did not really think of her when he said, "We have *made* love." Anabel, trembling, said, "That's the nicest thing anybody ever said to me."

She was also delighted that he was starting his tour in Kentucky. "And a monastery, of all places," she kept saying. He explained to her that St. Zachary's was a men's college attached to a monastery, but she preferred to think of him among the silent Trappists at

Gethsemane. She had read a lot about Trappists, and Thomas Merton, and cheese. "They make wonderful cheese," she said. "And they'll meet you at the airport in their black nighties."

"Nobody ever meets me at the airport, Anabel. I find my own way. And it's not Gethsemane. It's a school outside of Lexington." It was difficult not to lose patience with Anabel. But he was determined they would make love again before he left the apartment. He was successful, of course, enormously successful, but the project had taken patience. He did not like to have to be patient with people; he accepted them for what they were; the word *patience* assumed superiority, like the word *tolerance.* He often said so at college chapels and business clubs.

"I don't know so much about Lexington. I came from Western Kentucky." Anabel giggled so helplessly that she sloshed her champagne onto her white couch. "I have to laugh, you in a monastery. I bet you can tell them a two or thing."

But she was charming and her skin was lovely. The very idea of Ralph's telling the monks a two or thing seemed to increase her ardor. The third time they made love it was she who said, "We have *made* love." She was quite sober. Ralph preferred sober love. In an article, already anthologized, he had spoken against "America's tendency to find love in its cups." Still, he was almost overcome by the intensity and pathos of Anabel's sober love.

"You'll miss me in the monastery?" she asked in her entrance hall. Her eyes were large as she looked up at him. She wore a floating white negligee. He remembered clothes that Joan Crawford and Norma Shearer had worn a long time ago.

A moment ago he had been abrupt in his eagerness to get out of the foolish apartment that smelled of ashtrays and wine and Anabel Forsythe. Now he was loath to open the door into the long hall that stretched through October, past Kentucky, wandering among the Woman's Clubs whose aging officers belched under their magnificently ugly hats, and the colleges whose professors wanted help in getting their dissertations published, and the civic organizations whose membership meant to get around to reading your books.

"I'll miss you. I'll miss you, Anabel."

She moved away from him, and then into his arms. She was crying. Her face was not young.

"Here, here, Anabel. My God, baby. What's the matter, baby?"

She dug her fingernails into his shoulders before she said, "Go on," as Joan Crawford and Norma Shearer had said a long time ago.

"I'll see you Thanksgiving. I'll be back before Thanksgiving. I don't want to leave you like this."

"Please," she said. She was all right. She was smiling.

He was not insincere when he half closed his eyes and spoke of having made love. A man could not be called insincere merely because he looked and spoke as he had looked and spoken before. He did not want to be insincere. He was honestly fond of Anabel Forsythe. He reached for her.

"I'm fine. I'm just fine. You'll write me." She had moved around him. She stood at the opened door smiling. She patted his cheek. "Please go on."

"You're all right?"

"I'm wonderful."

At the end of the ridiculously long hall, he turned to wave at her, but she was not standing at her door, and he was relieved. She could have been standing in the center of the hall, lifting her white arm. Everything had been very fine with Anabel Forsythe.

But St. Zachary's was not just outside of Lexington. The man at the airport had never heard of the place. The Rent-A-Car girl had heard of it, though. "It's beautiful, just beautiful. My brother went there." She wore a gold cross at her neck. "*Where* is it beautiful?" Ralph asked, smiling because he needed to get in the habit of smiling. He smiled and smiled. He would smile his goddamned face off, from now to Thanksgiving.

"Oh, you mean where is it?" The girl laughed as if he had made a real humdinger of a joke.

He should have taken her advice and rented a car. But he disliked the responsibility of driving, and the expense. The old ladies at Consolidated Artists got him bigger fees than anybody in the country, while charging the same percentage they had charged Ralph Waldo Emerson and William Jennings Bryan. But they were smart toads; they made him take care of all his expenses. Most of the time he was a very smart toad, too; when he didn't have to take a limousine into Lexington, and a cab to the bus station—he had not known that the station was just around the corner—and then go to Berea, and then go to Waine, and then find another cab—buy another cab, really—for the next fifteen miles.

"Waine?" he said to the Rent-A-Car girl. "We are both still speaking of Kentucky, I assume."

He slayed the girl, she said so. If he had known how early he was going to arrive at St. Zachary's, he would have hung around the airport a little while. He could have rented a car and parked it up some horse-farm road by a white fence. Or maybe the girl had an apartment. She was pretty as a calendar, laughing, while her gold cross jiggled into her collar. Quite obviously she was as excitable as Anabel Forsythe, and young, ridiculously young.

Out of the cracked window of a twenty-year-old Chevrolet he looked at mountains and mist, scenery such as one found only at the conclusion of Hollywood films with a high sugar content. And there, above him, was St. Zachary's. Actually Ralph Clark drew in his breath. "It is breathtaking, absolutely," he would say to the Pope or the Abbot, or whoever turned out to be his host.

"There she is," the sullen driver said, turning into a narrow gravel road.

From the highway *she* was a marshmallow cathedral with spun sugar spires, prettier than a postcard. The church was set in a postcard emerald square, and behind it, still farther up the mountain, clung three or four other buildings, great white cubes of stone.

It was four o'clock in the afternoon. Twelve hours ago Anabel Forsythe said, "Please, go on," as if the words meant something. In the hills of Kentucky he was saying, "Turn around."

"I thought you said you wanted to go to St. Zach's?"

"I'm too early. I assumed the college was near a town."

"It ain't. I told you it ain't. That's St. Zach's."

"Take me back to Waine."

"You're the boss."

The man jerked the wheel angrily, turning his car in the middle of the road, barely missing the ditch. "Careful," Ralph said.

"I take care my end, you take care yours," the man said. His Adam's apple was monstrous. He swallowed three times before he said, "It'll be another ten dollars to come out again."

Ralph leaned back against the torn upholstery. He was trembling. He was actually trembling with anger at the simpleminded son of a bitch who had chosen this Sabbath day for robbery. Ralph swallowed too before he spoke, conscious of his own Adam's apple. "Very well," he said.

He swallowed before he said, "I need a drink. I tell you the truth, buddy." His voice sounded exactly like the driver's. It was a pleasant game, adopting the speech habits of people he met. But he would not honor this son of a bitch by copying him. He said, "I don't imagine the good fathers will offer me a drink. I failed to pack a flask." *When in Rome, and who ever gets out of Rome?* he always said to the old ladies of Consolidated when he came back to tell them about a tour. They loved to hear about his experiences; they wriggled in their straight chairs, and tittered, and covered their mouths with their handkerchiefs. He was the star of Consolidated Artists. Almost 30 percent of his assignments were return engagements. The old ladies couldn't compliment him enough.

"I'm a Methodist, a Free Methodist," the driver said. "You don't drink around here on Sunday, even if you Catlic. Everything closed tightern a drum."

Ralph would tell the old ladies: "I've never been amused by humorous cab drivers, even here in New York," although a couple of his speeches began with amusing cab drivers.

"You'll drop me at the hotel, then. Where I hailed you?"

The man did not answer.

Outside the car window the hills danced slowly in the mist. Outside, the hills were unbelievably lovely.

"I don't like what I'm doin' on Sunday. I'm doin' it for money. I need the money," the man was saying. "You want me come back get you?"

They were in front of the skinny stucco building where, a little while ago, Ralph had considered himself fortunate to find the taxi. The single picture window of Hotel Waine reflected the old Chevrolet and Ralph opening the car door, and Ralph's turning around for the luggage. The driver did not offer to help. He said, "I come back for ten dollars."

Ralph set the two suitcases and his attache case on the curb. He folded his topcoat over his arm. He was smiling before he turned again to the driver. He opened his billfold. "Ten dollars now, and when you come back . . ."

"Ten dollars again," the man said, extending his hand. Their hands touched. The driver's hand was moist and cold, but Ralph did not flinch at the contact. He was in thorough control. The old ladies were always expressing their amazement at his stamina. He had not failed an engagement in five years, come sleet, or storm, or cab driver.

He said, "I wouldn't cut off my nose to spite my face."

The man could have laughed. His hateful little ferret face could have turned friendly; they could have communicated together through a proverb.

"I wouldn't either," the man's hateful mouth said.

"Yes, please come back," Ralph said. "A little after six. Let's say six-fifteen."

The street was deserted. The car turned at the end of the block. The fact of the car disappeared with the sound of it. Across the street, Waine was a church and a hardware store and a grocery and a pick-up truck which held one empty burlap sack. Behind him, Waine, Kentucky, was a drugstore and the hotel. The drugstore was closed. The hotel was not closed; it was only deserted. The lobby, a small box, was crushed under its wallpaper of manure fleurs-de-lis. Four fat brown chairs looked at the picture window. Somebody had been reading *The Sunday Herald-Leader*; somebody had been smoking a cigar. Although Waine, Kentucky, had obviously been abandoned for the month of October, Ralph deposited his heavy luggage beside one of its brown chairs. He coughed several times before he said, "Hello, there." He did not expect to be answered, but he said, "Hello, there," again.

If he were weary of quaint cab drivers, he was even more weary of quaint old Negroes. He was destined, of course, to hear a thousand stories of quaint old Negroes from the Club ladies. Anabel had laughed gaily when he described the stories he would hear. "I know, I know," she said, leaning against him. He had not expected to be confronted by the old Negro himself, not so soon, not before the tour even began.

"Yassuh, yassuh, Mistah Dave jis step out a minute," the Negro said, straight from Uncle Remus. He rolled his eyes and bobbed his kinky head. He was all smiles and helpfulness. Yes indeed, the gennelman was welcome and wait for his ride.

But then it was no, suh, boss, and sorry boss. He'd got hisself in a peck of trouble once; they had local option, and it was Sunday besides; and he didden dare, much as he'd admire to accommodate the gennelman, but no suh, not even for fifteen dollars.

"It's a matter of necessity. It's a matter of my health." Ralph's voice was harsh. He made no effort to speak in the Negro's voice. "Twenty dollars. I'll give you twenty dollars for one bottle of Scotch. Now!"

"If it's that a way. If it's youah healf . . ." The old man was sidling away. He would be a little spell, but the drugstore would be opening up in a minute or two. The gentleman could go next door and have him some coffee. "I be back, don't you worry none."

"How long is a little spell?" Ralph asked loudly, but the old man had disappeared into the manure wallpaper.

He had not disappeared into the paper, of course. There was a door behind the desk, painted the color of the fleurs-de-lis. "The drug stoah," Ralph said. He had a good ear; he was proud of his ear.

The young girl behind the counter was not really the old Negro painted white and in another costume. She could have been, of course. Anything could happen in Kentucky. "We stay open hour mornin' evenin', but we don't han no sanniches." She grunted the words out. "We get sanniches in tomorrow. Miz Beecroft make him all wrapped in wax paph, and little names on what kind they are. We stay open perscription mostly, and I don' fill out the perscription. Max do. He just step out a minute."

Over and over the girl washed a glass. The short sleeves of her soiled blouse bit into her plump white arms. Ralph did not consider her body. He still felt horny. But he would no more consider her body than he would consider scaring himself with the idea that he and the old Negro were the only people left alive in the world. He was tired. He was goddamned tired, that was all. He was only goddamned tired. He thought of Anabel's arms reaching toward him.

And, of course, the foolish old Negro did not appear until the cab was honking outside. Ralph considered opening the package in the lobby, tearing into the bottle, standing in front of the picture window and drinking deep while the Free Methodist and Uncle Remus watched. But there wasn't time. There wasn't any point in taking the time. The bottle was wrapped in newspaper with dirty string.

"Mistah Buck's waitin'," the Negro said, pushing the bundle into Ralph's hands.

"You're sure there's a bottle inside all this wrapping? You're not trying to put one over on me?"

Yassuh and nosuh, and yassuh.

The Negro reached for the suitcases, but Ralph said, "Never mind." He took his time opening the attache case and placing the bottle inside with his speech cards. "You black son of a bitch," Ralph said.

"The son of a bitch," he said in the car.

They were out of town. It took less than a minute to leave Waine, Kentucky, behind you. And the driver was obviously the same man who had stopped in front of the hotel a couple of hours ago. The driver was more relaxed now; he wore his hunting cap at a little different angle; Waine, Kentucky, could not possibly boast taxi driving twins.

The son of a bitch cleared his throat for three or four miles. Then, without any possible reason, he said, "I was a little riled. I didn't mean to give you a hard time, Mister. I wasn't nice. I tell you . . ." The twin taxi-driver was determined to tell the story of his whole goddamned life, and why he needed money, even though he was getting his goddamned money. "And beside, I been out there just afore I picked you up. A fellow decided to change his mind and not go. You see, I was eating at you because . . .

"How long you aimin' to stay?"

"Until Wednesday afternoon." Ralph spoke carefully over his anger, determined that the man should not annoy him.

"You see, you see . . ." the son of a bitch said, and finally, finally, St. Zachary stood above them in the green light of the October evening.

"Like I said, no hard feelings." The man took the sharp curves without caution. "I don't like for the sun to go down on my wrath."

"And keep your goddamned witnessing to yourself," Ralph said.

The humorous cab driver shrugged his shoulders. "Like I said," he said, and "Here we are."

They had stopped in the middle of the pavement. Behind them the cathedral stood lavender in the light. Beside them reared a dark wall. Ahead, boys in white shirts moved easily over a bright patch of lawn. The lighting was outrageously theatrical.

"You want me come back for you Wednesday?" The man was actually opening the car door. He was reaching for the suitcases.

"Hell." Ralph was determined to be civil. He was not superstitious. But he had often found that the first stop of a tour determined the tone of the whole series. "Spend New Year's day in work and cheer, and you'll be happy all the year," Muriel used to say. She believed it, too. Muriel tried to believe everything in the whole goddamned world.

"I didn't mean to swear at you back there. I'm just tired," Ralph said.

"Sure, we all get tired." The twin held the suitcases. "You can call me. I'm in the book. Just Buck's Taxi Service."

"I'm on a lecture tour," Ralph said, placing eleven dollars into the man's shirt pocket. "They're always grueling."

"Sure," the man said, and "Thanks." He did not check the money. "I don't know which door you go in, but they'll find you." The man's laughter was a quick cackle.

"Yeah, yeah, sure," Ralph said, and the taxi scratched backwards down the drive.

The dark building was like a penitentiary, stretching a city block or more. But the cathedral was still there, all right. And ahead the squares of white stone showed glass faces to the green.

He had started to enter the door of the penitentiary beside him. But a discreet white piece of cardboard said in black capital letters:

NO ADMITTANCE
(LADIES ABSOLUTELY PROHIBITED)
MONASTIC ENCLOSURE

For some goddamned reason he was embarrassed by the sign. He whistled under his breath a little, as if he had meant only to look at the door, not enter it. He folded his topcoat, placing it and the case under his left arm. He stooped to pick up the suitcases. Anabel would be delighted with the letter about the funny sign. The suitcases were ridiculously heavy.

He would begin his main address with compliments to the fathers, the student body, the scenery, the cathedral, something, something, and I am charmed that St. Zachary proves its catholicity by taking to its bosom all architecture, including my own.

The dark pavement was long, almost as long as Anabel's hall. He was hot. His shirt stuck to his back. He moved awkwardly, banging the suitcases against his legs. A penitentiary examined cases of conscience, and a penitentiary was a house of correction. But he could hardly use that information to begin a speech and soften up the bastards of St. Zachary.

Perspiration ran into his eyes. Three white shirts blurred against the grass still in the sun. The end of the penitentiary was dark as a cave. He set down the suitcases. He took his carefully folded handkerchief from his breast pocket and wiped his forehead. He was breathing awkwardly. One of the white shirts moved from the grass and toward Ralph Clark, and past him. Perhaps the boy nodded. Perhaps the son of a bitch spoke, but Ralph was not sure.

The end of the penitentiary actually held a kind of cave. It was a portecochere, like the one at Muriel's parents' house in Overbrook, or like a funeral home in some bloody little midwestern town. Two priests stood together in the shadows. The thin one wore a slouched hat and smoked a cigarette, like Humphrey Bogart in a late movie. The taller one smoked a cigar with a red band on it. Anabel had been wrong. They did not wear black nighties. Their outfits were straight black tailored bathrobes, and very goddamned becoming, as they no doubt knew. The two men in their handsome clothes gave no indication of seeing Ralph, although he stood within ten feet of them. He cleared his throat, and they continued their low-voiced conversation. He had to come right up to the sucks before they admitted that his mortal body existed.

"I'm Ralph Clark from the Consolidated Bureau," he said, putting down his luggage again.

They turned slowly. "Oh?" the Cigar Priest said.

"I'm here to visit the campus for a couple of days."

"Yes?"

"I'm here to speak." The men had obviously never heard of him. For an angry moment Ralph remembered fainting. He had fainted once in Korea. He had made over thirty thousand dollars from the experience, an article and the sale of the title to some Hollywood doofs. It was a neat little piece about refusing to face life, and then facing it. But here, fainting, or any display of emotion, would be shameful.

Neither of the men introduced himself. Perhaps they did not know their names. Perhaps they had no names. Perhaps it was an affectation of the order, going about so selfless and serving and handsome that they didn't need to be called anything, the sons of bitches.

"You'll excuse us," the Cigar Priest said to Humphrey Bogart, and Humphrey nodded without removing the cigarette from his mouth. "Father Dominic's around here some place. If you'll follow me."

"Very well." Ralph stooped for the suitcases.

"I'll help with those," the taller priest said, but of course Ralph said, "I have them all right. I'm determined to carry my own weight," which the priest considered very funny.

The lobby of the penitentiary looked like any subway station that had been prettied up with a few virgins and crucifixes. It smelled like mushrooms and old melons. But the waiting room was a surprise, full of low blonde chairs and tall thin lamps and a vast tan coffee table curving in front of the couch not unlike Anabel's, and, in the far corner, a desk with a tan telephone. "If you'll excuse me," the priest said. He had not thrown away his cigar. "I can't imagine where Father Dominic is. You will excuse me."

Ralph lowered his suitcases to the slick floor. He pretended to smile at the priest who dialed the telephone with a bright gold pencil. Ralph moved heavily to one of the chairs. He was feeling rocky. He imagined he could hear the telephone ringing out on the grass. Or the Cigar Priest was only playing with a stage telephone. He held the receiver away from his ear and smiled and smiled, showing his beautiful fat teeth. He was young, and fat.

"I can't imagine where he is. I'll call him again in a minute." Smiling he turned the cigar between his fat fingers over the glass top of the desk. "It's hot, isn't it?"

"Yes, very hot." Ralph sighed but he kept smiling. "It shouldn't be this hot in October." He closed his eyes. At least he had arrived. He would have liked to have sat quietly for a long time. But Cigar Priest said, "This may interest you."

From a drawer of the desk he produced a baseball. And why not a baseball? The man was a magician in a stage show, sitting beside a stage telephone. "Catch," the priest said.

Ralph dropped the ball, hating his clumsiness. He hated the priest's asthmatic laughter.

"I'll say," Ralph said. The glaring white ball was autographed. The light in the room was bad. He did not want to get out his reading glasses. And even if he could have read the autographs, he might not have recognized the names, renaissance man or not. For a moment he could not remember who had won the World Series.

But one did not have to respond to the jolly priest. "An old boy sent it to me last week. I knew Father Killian would want it for his museum. He said for me to keep it a while, and I told him it would get dirty. Father Killian really wants this ball." The story was almost too funny for the priest to tell. He was holding another baseball in his hand. Well, this morning, Father Lawrence gave me this old dirty ball. He told me to remind Father Killian I'd told him to take it if he wanted it. And I told him it would get dirty. Well, this morning, when Father Killian dropped by . . ."

The story was impossible to follow. Funny Priest held the dirty ball over the desk, laughing until tears stood in his eyes.

Ralph thought of throwing the white ball back across the space between them. Instead, he placed the ball carefully on the coffee table, steadying it against a neat pile of pamphlets. Then he lighted a cigarette. He was so tired his hands were trembling.

"Oh my, I wish you could have seen his face." The priest rubbed at his eyes before he began another foolish story about football practice and a young priest who surely wasn't named Father Clara, but the fat man was saying "Father Clara." Everybody was a funny priest who played football and Bing Crosby, and rode bicycles, and went swimming in their cassocks.

"I'll declare." It was sufficient response.

"I was showing them how to kick. I coached football when I came here. The first year was the only time St. Zachary ever had a winning team. That was thirty years ago."

"Impossible." Ralph spoke involuntarily.

"How's that?"

"You couldn't have come here thirty years ago."

"I was younger then," the priest said, chuckling as he dialed the telephone, smiling, smiling, smiling, as the bell sounded.

"You're not old enough to have come here that long ago."

"Who's not old enough?" The man rose gracefully. He moved gracefully around the table, his skirts whispering. "I'll just have to go find him. You don't mind waiting." The band on his cigar smouldered. "It looks as if I'm about to burn myself up." He leaned over the ashtray in front of Ralph to stub out his cigar.

"You don't mind if I read your propaganda?"

Ralph had not meant to amuse the old priest. "Go right ahead." The man laughed until he coughed. "That's what it's there for." And then he went out of the room, closing the door after him, which was a crazy thing for him to do. If this were the reception room (and why shouldn't it be?), what was Ralph Clark doing in it with the door closed, needing, Oh God, a drink, and some sleep, and Oh God needing.

One of the papers was a school bulletin named *The Zacharinian*, mimeographed in purple ink, with, yes God, bowling scores of teams named, yes, The Bunnies, and yes, Powerful Pioneers. One was a badly printed little booklet on bad paper, published in Georgia (in a real penitentiary?) entitled, "An Adolescent's Prayer to the Blessed Mother"; the last lines said, they honestly said: "At the time of my death I will have my Mother's lap to bury my head in." That was actually what it said. Ralph reached under his jacket to unstick his shirt. He could not even remember his mother's face. On the rare occasions he tried to recall her, he could muster only a couple of pictures in a newspaper. At the time of her death she had been working on a paper in Seattle. He and Muriel were traveling in Italy, and they hadn't known about it until two weeks after the funeral. They hadn't known about his father's death either. He could not recall his father's face.

There was an address from the Pope to somebody, and an order blank where you could get a pink picture of Jesus and a subscription to a magazine and a blessing for only three dollars, which was pretty goddamned cheap. The Cigar Priest was right about everything; everything was pretty goddamned funny.

Ralph was pleased to find a slick poop publication about St. Zachary. The pictures were stunning. It was always nice to look at pictures of where you sat. And there was some of the information he would have already known if he hadn't been so busy with Anabel. Seven hundred students. St. Zachary's considered man's reason as the noblest natural gift of God, and there were two pages on financial arrangements, explaining a Pay as You Go plan. It cost four thousand lousy dollars a year to attend their bugging school where they shut you up in a hot room and left you. For two cents he could get his ass off their couch and get the hell out.

The man knocked before he came in. He waited until Ralph said "Come in" three times. The man was quite tall, as tall as Ralph, but thinner. He looked a little like Eisenhower in his last Washington days, or Ralph's father, or anybody's father. He extended his hand. He said, "I'm Dominic Baker," as if the name meant something to Ralph, which it didn't. At least he didn't call himself *Father.* At least he was a relief after Laughing Fat. He stood in the sweltering room and asked polite questions. He listened politely. He was not smiling, but he was not unsmiling either. "Yes, I had a good trip. Yes, I've eaten," Ralph lied. "No, my bags aren't in my room." Ralph gestured to his luggage in the corner.

"I'm sure you're tired. If you would like to retire now . . ."

"Yes, yes, please."

The man stooped to pick up the suitcases. "I'll get those," Ralph said, but the man was already at the door. "This is fine," the man said, and Ralph had to hurry to keep up with him.

They did not go back to the portecochere. They made their way through the long building. The hall was dim. At a sudden turn a bright face appeared in the wall, batting her eyes against the candle that burned before her. A door opened into the soft October evening. Father Dominic held the door with one of the suitcases. He was breathing heavily. "We go straight ahead."

"Please, it's my turn to carry."

"Very well," the old man said. "And I take your coat and bag."

It was not a single building. It was many buildings. Fortunately the man slowed his pace.

To their left doors moved past, leading to offices? class rooms? the men's john? Pope's John: a place to pray or be sick? and into the evening again, and back to another wide dim hall, like an illustration for perspective, glistening, smelling of oil and antiseptic, with a wall of doors and a wall for the blinking faces: the Virgin, the Virgin, a Bearded Man, the Virgin; doors even barred the halls themselves; Father Dominic held the doors open; they were outside again, Father Dominic holding the door. They were both breathing heavily as if they had run a mile or made love.

The last door held the sign again:

NO ADMITTANCE
(LADIES ABSOLUTELY PROHIBITED)
MONASTIC ENCLOSURE

"I'm staying in the monastery?"

Father Dominic moved ahead down the last oiled sea of the hall which now held doors on either side. Every door held a large white card as carefully printed as the No Admittance sign: REV. FR. CONNALL, REV. FR. MATTHEW, REV. FR. BEDE, REV. FR. ARNOLD, REV. FR. URWIN.

At the end of the hall a door said MR. RALPH CLARK.

The name was written in black ink, in longhand. It was Ralph's name. The writing was not like Muriel's, but he saw the name in Muriel's handwriting on the envelopes of the letters she wrote to Paris, and Cairo, and Johannesburg, after he had insisted that she stop traveling with him, after everything was long gone done, and she was still too stubborn to admit that everything was long gone done. Right up to the divorce Muriel was going to save their marriage. She was going to save him. "From what? For what?" he shouted at her. "Yourself. Us," she shouted back, as if she really had something on her mind.

Father Dominic stepped back. He gestured at the door. Ralph nodded. Father Dominic's thin hand opened the door. Even before the door swung open, Ralph knew that Muriel waited in the room.

It was huge. Two windows with dark green blinds stood over the long radiator. By the green leather chair stood a floor lamp with, yes God, velvet pulls. And there was a glass ashtray on a metal stand. The rug was flowered roses. The bed, Ralph knew before he turned, was mahogany with pineapple posts. A thin-legged table beside it held, yes, a goosenecked lamp.

Father Dominic placed the case on the bench of the vanity dresser: its three mirrors were shaped like church windows. And they reflected the bed. It was difficult to keep from laughing at the bed in the mirror just as it had waited in the mirror at Muriel's house. "A whorehouse, Ralph, the very idea," Muriel said the first night they moved into the vast back room. "Oh, really, Ralph," she said, kissing him.

Father Dominic had turned on the vanity lamps, the floor lamp, the goosenecked lamp by the bed. "Will this be all right?" In the bright lights of the room he looked suddenly younger. It was impossible to tell the ages of the religious or the mad; it was utterly impossible. In her own way Muriel had been both mad and religious.

"It's fine. It's very nice," Ralph said, trying to remember a voice he used with the presidents of the clubs. A lecturer was asked to return, not for what he said, but for his graciousness. "It's a lovely room. It reminds me of a room I lived in once, for a while," Ralph said, not knowing how to stop the sentence, "for a year, in fact for almost two years. In Philadelphia."

The priest smiled. He did not seem to mind the quiet of the room. He would have stood there with his goddamned smile if Ralph had let the sentence run on and on and on. She was rich.

And she was very crazy about moral and spiritual values. And she helped her husband. At first she helped her husband. "Will you . . . won't you sit down?" Ralph asked, not remembering any voice to use. He lowered the suitcases carefully, as if they held his head.

The priest's spare body sat in a single movement on the vanity bench.

"This chair," Ralph said.

"Of course not. You've had the long trip."

There was the quiet again. Father Dominic smiled. The only sound was the pounding of Ralph's head, or the sea of the hall outside, or Muriel's heart against his ear.

"I'm . . . I'm afraid I'm rather vague about this engagement. The people at the agency generally brief me, but . . ."

"We are just starting our program here. We are a young school. We feel our way." The priest waited.

A speaker speaks, Ralph Clark always said. The old ladies were always quoting him to their new artists. They were very motherly old ladies. Ralph Clark says a speaker asks some questions, but mostly he speaks, from the minute he meets the reception committee until he leaves.

"This is a new experience for me. I have never visited a Catholic school before—not for any reason, it has just so happened. And I have never stayed in a monastery before." The priest's smile did not change. "I assume I am being sponsored by your Department of American Studies . . . Generally when I visit colleges, I talk to several classes, in addition to the public address . . . You are in American Studies? The History Department?"

"Yes, I suppose so. I teach one class, in the spring semester."

"You are an administrator?"

The priest appeared uneasy. At least once during the visit he had the grace to appear uneasy. "I'm . . . they call me the president."

"Oh, I'm sorry."

"Sometimes I'm sorry, too. There are many problems in administration."

Into the silence Ralph said, "Of course, I'm sure, I'm sure." And he said, "We could talk about the state of my soul, or my assignments for the next two days."

"Your assignments, by all means. We are not Jesuit," the priest said, which was a crazy goddamned thing to say.

It was a painful conversation. I am talking to Father Dominic of St. Zachary's College. There is a convocation at eleven on Tuesday. I am lighting a cigarette. The boys of the school are chiefly interested in Business Administration. Many of them go on to the Harvard Business School. I am listening carefully. The teachers with whom I will be associated are named: the nature of the monastic life is: the problems of administration are:

He would have been glad to talk about religion. He had gone to church with his mother, on occasion. He had been quite upset once, for a little while, fearing that he was not saved. He had cried in the night, and his mother had tried to comfort him. One day Jesus was looking over Ralph Clark, and the next day Ralph was looking over himself. He was not positive he really remembered the crying in the night. He had tried to remember in order to comfort Muriel, whose tormented mind was often difficult to understand. "I believe. I believe something," Muriel said. "Help me, Ralph."

"It's ridiculous how much this room is like that other room," Ralph said, surprised at his voice. "My wife always wanted everything to *mean*, even coincidences."

"Coincidences are always happening," the priest said, rising, and Ralph could not remember the man's name. "I suppose everything *can't* mean." He stood at a door near the bed. "Your bathroom is in here."

"Of course," Ralph said, pushing himself to his feet.

"I'll call for you in the morning for breakfast."

"Fine, fine." He could call the priest Father. He did not need to remember any of their names. He could call them all Father. Even if he did not have the energy to curse the man smiling at the door he could say, "Goodnight, Father."

He leaned his head against the closed door. He waited until the priest's footsteps disappeared into the water. He turned the brass key stealthily. It made only the smallest click. He barely heard it himself. He took the Scotch from his case. The strings came off easily. He folded the newspaper into a neat square and placed it in the wicker wastebasket by the door.

The bathroom was larger than their bathroom. The marble walls and the partitions for the toilet and bathtub were of gray marble instead of pink. Beside the priests' old-fashioned bathtub was a chenille mat instead of the square of carpet from the bedroom. But there was the same mirror, and the same wooden chests of different heights on the window wall.

"We have *made* love," Muriel said the night they had been married by a justice of the peace, after the scene with her parents, after they had gone up to the big room on the third floor, after they had made love. But there was no logic in her. Even that first night she had insisted that it was perfectly fine and righteous for them to live in her parents' house and eat her parents' food as long as they needed to, until Ralph's writing got recognized. "It's right. It's the only right thing in the world. What's food worth?" He said, "Not so loud." She pulled away from him laughing. "You don't have to be quiet when you have *made* love," she said.

For a long time, ever since the divorce, he had not thought about that night. It was a good night, and it was very goddamned crazy not to remember it. Except some of it was very goddamned silly to remember. Remembering had nothing to do with moral and spiritual values.

Afterwards, in the bathroom, he had taken her lipstick and drawn a heart on the pink marble wall of the bathtub enclosure. She was taking another bath, for God's sake. He put their initials in the heart. He said, "You are love." That is what he said, serious as all hell, and twenty-five goddamned years old, and she looked at him, oh my God, and nobody was laughing. She said, "Maybe I am. And you are, too. We are love," she said, rising from the funny old bathtub. He thought of Venus rising from the sea. My God, he said it. He said, "You are Venus rising from the sea," to that scrawny body in that goddamned bathroom a thousand frigging years ago. And Muriel wanted him to leave the initials on the wall, for Christ sake. The next morning she sat on the edge of the tub and said, "Please don't Ralph. Kilroy's here. Please, Ralph, it's terribly important to be Kilroy."

He slanted the tumbler over the priest's lavatory bowl. He poured his drink quietly, adding an inch of water. He placed three aspirin in the palm of his hand. He watched himself take the aspirin in the mirror. He poured and drank again, without water, toasting himself. He took the third drink back into the bedroom and placed it on the spindle-legged table. Then he undressed in the vanity mirror that also reflected the bed. He had a good body, firm and tight-stomached. It was a young black-haired body in all three of the mirrors.

He put on his pajamas and robe before he went into the toilet stall. The priests' walls had never been written on. He kept thinking it would be pretty fine to write on the priests' walls, a few pictures and rhymes and specifications and Anabel's telephone number. He laughed in the bathroom stall thinking about it. He damn near laughed aloud.

He brushed his teeth.

He sat in the leather chair with his attache case beside him. He was fine. The headache would go away in a minute and he would be very fine. It was just that he had not slept decently in the past week. "This may interest you," he should have said to Laughing Cigar. "I have slept indecently for the past three nights. And I will rise again."

"You may come in now, Muriel," he said, but not aloud of course. He only whispered the words. For almost two years he had stopped his mind when it began to think about Muriel. He had stopped his mind for not any goddamned reason in the world except it was embarrassing. But he was almost forty-two years old, and you could sit in a chair and laugh when you were almost forty-two goddamned years old.

In his attache case his three-by-five speech cards were in fine order. Contemporary Man Is. Twentieth Century. America Is. He could speak the cards well, making them sound inspired for the particular moment. He would perform well. He had performed remarkably with Anabel. Brotherhood Is.

"Muriel."

But there wasn't anything to think. Sweet Jesus, he wanted to think about her.

She was thin and eager, and she had little sayings about New Year's Day and love; she lived in a house with a portecochere; she was clean and tailored, and she wanted their initials left on a bathtub stall.

On a far hill a dog barked. His stomach growled like a dog, loud enough to wake Rev. Fr., and Rev. Fr., and Rev. Fr. who lay behind their white cards facing their mirrors. They lay in the beds they had made, but Jesus, Jesus Christ, their beds wouldn't stay made. Muriel refused to come into the room.

He threw out his hand. The stand of the ashtray rocked and teetered, and then it fell with a great clatter. He held his breath to listen. But the sound had not broken the ashtray. It was a fine heavy piece of glass in the metal stand. He knelt. Using one of his notecards for a broom and one for a dustpan he cleaned the rug thoroughly. No one would ever know that he had spilled an ashtray on the floor. The penitentiary was like any other quiet hotel. If he listened carefully he could hear footsteps outside. But his hall was not being patrolled. It was only the sounds of any night, in any hotel. He could hear, if he tried, a radio playing dance music, or chanting. But he didn't have to listen. The sounds could listen to him if anything wanted to hear anything. Any experience was *the* experience, which was pretty much fine enough for any goddamned twentieth-century renaissance man. Laughing Cigar or Rent-A-Car girl.

The door knocked. The knock at the door was an experience.

He could make his way across the room. He could unlock the door without being ashamed he had locked it. He could hold to the doorknob and stand very straight and say, "Hello, Father."

"I'm sorry. I didn't know you had retired."

"Fine, fine. I'm just going over my notes for tomorrow."

"I failed to ask what time you will want to have your breakfast."

"Any time, any time. When in Rome . . ." The priest still waited. "Seven-thirty, eight?"

"You will want to sleep," the priest who was any age said. "I'll collect you at eight-thirty."

"Fine, fine," Ralph said. "I'll be glad to be collected." His voice was not mocking. He was not even annoyed with the good black father in his uniform.

"Goodnight."

"Goodnight, Father." He was sorry he could not remember the mother-loving old bastard's name.

The wood of the door was cool against his forehead.

He could call Buck to come after him. There wasn't any telephone in the room, just the black crucifix over the bed which he hadn't even bothered to notice. But he could find his way down the halls to the waiting room and the tan telephone. Or, he could take his pencil and write on the walls of the toilet. He could write Jesus Saves and Muriel Saves. Or, he could knock the ashtray over, and pull over the vanity dresser. He could do almost any goddamned thing he wanted to. And everything was almost too funny to think about. But he did not laugh aloud. Even if Rev. Fr. Poopface had patrolled the sea outside, he would not have heard Ralph laughing.

After a while he focused his eyes on his very elegant goddamned wristwatch which somebody had given him, he couldn't remember where. He had spent a full week at the school, and they had paid him thirty-two hundred dollars, and they gave him the watch to boot, and the girl, who was a very nice little piece, cried when she made the presentation. It was only ten o'clock. He hadn't gone to sleep at ten o'clock in a thousand years. He slept like a baby straight through to eight o'clock, in the bathtub, of all the goddamned places.

The visit to St. Zachary's turned out splendidly. Ralph Clark had come to the school never having heard of it; he left feeling a real friendship even for St. Zachary himself. He visited a number of classes in American Studies, History, and English. He spoke to the convocation. He conducted at least four informal seminars. He was particularly impressed by the school's liberal attitudes. The members of the administration, staff, and student body were, without exception, kind, eager, and cooperative.

Both Monday and Tuesday evenings, before dinner, several of the priests and Ralph had manhattans in the office of the Chairman of the English Department. The priests enjoyed Ralph's story of the old Negro. The Cigar Priest laughed until tears came to his eyes.

Ralph Clark was so involved with St. Zachary's that he almost missed the bus from Waine to Lexington. He failed to call Buck's Taxi Service until only an hour before the bus was due. A woman, sounding almost hysterical, said that Buck was sick, but she would try to send somebody. She said, "Buck's mighty bad off." The old car finally came, with no time to spare. The driver was a callow youth of bad complexion. The back of his neck was as soft as a girl's. He was, fortunately, noncommunicative.

Ralph could not imagine why he had been disturbed the night of his arrival. During his entire visit at St. Zachary he had not thought of Muriel at all. He did not even think of Anabel, the slut, the whore, the bitch.

Love

Lately I am very interested in the word *love*, since next year I will be a junior in high school. It is a word which is rather popular in our family. My mother uses it a great deal, and so does my father, even, when he's at home. My grandmother does not say it quite so much, but I guess she says it more than an average person. We live with my grandmother or my grandmother lives with us—it depends upon whom you are talking to. I said, "We live with my maternal grandmother," so I suppose I am on her side. I am named Alice for her and our home is, of course, in Kentucky.

My mother says over and over that you don't take sides in a family. She keeps saying we are one adoring unit. I suppose she includes Bud when she says it because she turns her head and she spreads her hands as if she meant everybody. Bud is a very light Negro and lives by himself in the servant's cottage behind our house. Perhaps my mother does not really love Bud. But no matter who's visiting us and asking questions, the way people do, my mother says, "We love each other very much." When she spreads her hands that way the bracelets on her arm tinkle like the wind chimes. She's always telling Dr. Thaxton she loves him for giving Grandmother her insulin shots, for instance. It may be my imagination, but I keep thinking my mother's perfume smells more when she says the word *love* to Dr. Thaxton. I guess it is because she is generally moving her body and the perfume escapes, as it were.

Although my mother is very lovely and fragile, I do not think she ever considers the different meanings of words a great deal. Last month she was very upset when I told her I was in love with Mr. Grask who taught our literature class. I would say the same thing again if we ever talked about him. But I guess it is just as well he won't be coming back next fall—my mother is on the school board. I will not ever forget Mr. Grask who decided me to become a creative writer, and I will always love him. I realize he was not expensive looking like my father, and I realize his background was not too much. Still, I remember him very often, and I have talked to my grandmother about him lately, now that it is summer.

My grandmother says I have a fine attitude about Mr. Grask. The first day I mentioned him to her she said it would be wrong if I ever stopped remembering him. She said love was a touching of the hands which is the sort of thing old women like to say. I do not believe my grandmother has lost her mind, though. She is practical, just the way I am: I never much thought about being married to Mr. Grask. I also do not believe my grandmother means to leave absolutely everything to Bud. Even if she does, I do not think she is crazy. I differ with my mother on this point, but we can not talk about it. I am sure Dr. Thaxton agrees with Mother. My father, on the other hand, is just an interested bystander, as this account will prove.

This afternoon my mother said it was difficult to believe I was her daughter. "I love you. I love you both so very much," my mother said. She was standing just inside Grandmother's bedroom door, but I could smell the perfume clear across the room. I weigh considerably more than my mother. Perhaps that is the reason she looked so small to me across the room. I was sorry I had stood up when she came in. My mother said, "You were plotting, I know you were. I can't bear it if you don't tell me what you were talking about."

"I've told you, Dorothy Elizabeth. That spring forty-three years ago." She smiled, and she said, "Forty-three years," a second time. My father is somewhat younger than my mother.

I think my grandmother tells stories very well, and I do not mind hearing them over and over. Several times lately she has remembered the spring my mother and Bud were born. The story begins with laughing; then my grandmother says, "Every blessed thing in the world was pregnant—sheep, and horses, and Hannah and me." She tells all about Hannah having Bud out back, and Mother being born here the next day. The end of the story is where the collie, named Lady, has nine puppies under the piano in the parlor. It is a funny story and full of spring, as I tried to tell my mother this afternoon, although I should not have sounded so poetic about it.

"It is not a poetic story, Alice," my mother said, "and I know you were plotting, both of you. I heard you say Bud's name."

"Just about the time he was born," my grandmother said. "Forty-three years ago."

"Honestly, Mother." My mother turned her head from side to side. "I've asked you not to dwell on sex. A thousand times I've asked you."

I do not like to see my mother upset, and I was sorry when my grandmother said, "I told every item about Lady and her family." My mother does not like to admit that I am not a child any more. I do not mind so much, because my grandmother says it is very nice to be "functioning properly," which is the way she expresses it. I did not look at my mother.

She said, "You're obscene, you're utterly obscene," and she went out of the room. Before this afternoon my mother often told my grandmother that she was *vulgar*, but she always took it back with other words like *darling* or *my precious love*. The word *obscene* sounded rather ugly.

My grandmother called after my mother. "Go back to my kitchen and tell Bud to bring the car around." Of course my mother did not answer, but in a minute she was walking across the back yard to Bud's door. Bud lives in the whole cottage now that my mother has moved the kitchen inside and Hannah has died. My grandmother yanked out the telephone wires the day the inside kitchen was finished, and she said my mother had to get another cook because Bud was quitting now that his mother was dead. Bud, incidentally, was a splendid cook. My grandmother sends my mother with messages to Bud rather often now that the telephone is out; also, we're always changing cooks.

My mother had to knock a number of times before Bud's door opened. I guess he was asleep. He sleeps a great deal during the day since he doesn't work any more. My mother beat on his door with both fists, and my grandmother said, "That ought to wake even Hannah," and she laughed. Although I am used to the way she talks, I did not laugh with her. I felt rather cold, I guess, because my mother looked very small down in the back yard.

My grandmother said, "I wonder if Dorothy Elizabeth ever wearies of her improvements." I didn't answer, because I really love my mother, and I do not like to talk about her.

I pushed the curtains apart just to have something to do, and my mother stopped knocking for a minute and looked up at me over her shoulder. I wish I could have thought of something to call to her. I waved, though. I'm not sure she really saw me. Her body was very tight, and she turned around and lifted her arms, but the door opened before she could knock again.

By the time Grandmother had gone to the bathroom Bud was honking out front. No matter what you say about him, he can dress very quickly. Naturally I don't know but what he was already dressed, but often he isn't. Bud has a great many friends who visit him of both sexes. My grandmother has always said that Bud's friends are his own business, which is something else that infuriates my mother. Grandmother says Bud is just naturally social, but I don't think she really believes it.

In the downstairs hall my father said, "So you ladies are out for another airing?" I smiled politely at him, and I thanked him for opening the screen for us. My father and I have always been polite to each other, since we do not know each other very well. He is usually gone most of the time judging horse shows and visiting various people. He has just come home from Miami, and I am quite interested in him now. He is good looking for a man of his age, as I have said. If I were my mother I would prefer him to Dr. Thaxton, but of course I'm not my mother. My father still has all his hair. I wish I had noticed him more this afternoon, but I didn't.

I don't remember whether my grandmother spoke to my father or not, but she generally does. At the time I did not know that today was going to be a day to make a personal story of, so I probably missed several things that could be fairly important. I am sure my grandmother called to Bud, "Don't you bother to get out." My grandmother always says that, for Bud is rather arrogant and sarcastic sometimes, and she respects him.

I walked very slowly behind my grandmother so she could open the door for herself. She does not like to be fussed over. The car is a limousine and very extravagant; it still smells new, although it is over a year old. When the door is opened you can smell it. The unusual part about this afternoon was that my grandmother opened the front door and scooted herself over beside Bud and patted the seat beside her. She was breathing rather heavily, but she said, "Hurry," and she said, "We'll all ride with Bud; it will be cozier." All of this, of course, took longer to act out than it does to tell, and I thought about several things before I closed the door, including the brotherhood of man which Mr. Grask was always talking about in literature class. I had not thought much about loving everybody before Mr. Grask, for Bud has always been a member of our family, but we never rode in the front seat with him.

I am not sure but I think my father called to us as I closed the car door. I was thinking about my father, too, as well as about Hannah being dead, and love, and several other things which don't fit together very well. When I'm thinking about Mr. Grask and it is lovely summer I think about a great many things at one time. My father smiled, anyhow.

"Don't spare the horses," my grandmother said as usual.

"Yes, Miss Alice," Bud said rather coldly, and we started off swiftly, just as usual.

In fact the whole ride was as usual, I guess, all the way to Lexington which is thirteen miles from our front door. It is the drive we always take, sometimes twice a day when it is lovely summer. The windows and ventilators are all open and the air blows loud and sweet against us, and Grandmother says, "Wheee" as we round the curve by Dr. Thaxton's tenant house. The speedometer needle moves to seventy and hangs like a silver fish, and the clean farms and the white fences fly past us, and I try to see everything all at once; and then we are turning around at the Gulf service station at the city limits of Lexington. It is all a little pattern we have worked out, and the only difference was being in the front seat, but it wasn't very different.

Going back wasn't very different, either, to tell the truth. I never look at anything coming back, because I've already seen it. Grandmother and I always talk some, the way we did today, and sometimes Bud will say something or other, but not always. He wasn't really arrogant this afternoon, but just inside himself. I sometimes think Bud is flying seventy miles an hour inside and doesn't have time to talk.

The real difference about yesterday was that I could see the side of Bud's face instead of the back of his head. I've been thinking about it, and I guess that is the main difference, not our talk. Bud is very handsome. His hair is cut close and his color is, as I said, light. It is hard to say exactly what his color is. I would say jersey-cow color, but Mr. Grask always said you shouldn't compare things to things which give a different meaning. I could say a dark peach, but that is not exactly right either. I was thinking about Bud's color and the shape of his nose which is more like mine than like Hannah's when she was alive. I guess I was feeling rather related to Bud. I am not saying that I think for sure Bud was my grandfather's son, but it is something which I have thought about. A person around Central Kentucky is always hearing stories, and everybody wonders about things. If I had known my grandfather I suppose I wouldn't wonder, but you do wonder about people who have killed themselves with a gun before you are born. It doesn't seem disloyal to wonder, and Hannah was the one who told me most about my grandfather —she said he was a saint. Hannah liked to talk as much as Bud likes not to talk. Anyhow, that is what I was thinking. I was not listening to my grandmother particularly. I thought a little about the time I told Mr. Grask that Bud was probably my uncle. Mr. Grask ran his hand through his hair and his eyes were white looking, and he put his hand on my shoulder and said I was a remarkably fine person, which I appreciated. He said it one day after debate practice. We were in his classroom in the basement together.

Although I was thinking all these things, I heard my grandmother say, "Sometimes it is very satisfactory to be an old woman and I don't mind anybody knowing how old I am." She punched me, and I said, "Of course not."

I nodded my head several times, but I kept looking at Bud. I was really wondering about Bud and the word love. I was not exactly thinking about Mr. Grask, except in the way you always think about somebody who has changed the way you think.

My grandmother said, "Alice was in love last spring, did you know that, Bud?"

Bud did not move his face at all, which is more embarrassing than if he had answered. Perhaps that is the meaning of arrogant. I do not approve of blushing, but I know when I'm doing it because my neck gets very hot and the palms of my hands feel funny. I did not stop looking at Bud, though; I didn't want my grandmother to know I was angry or embarrassed. Sometimes my grandmother is obscene, as my mother said, and she likes to embarrass people. I couldn't help blushing, but I could keep my eyes on Bud, and I felt more related to him than ever.

"Look, she's blushing," my grandmother said, and she laughed.

I said to myself that she was an old woman who wasn't responsible. It is something my mother has often said, but I said it myself. I said out loud, "Why do we always ride back so slowly?"

"She's changing the subject." My grandmother punched me, and I suppose she punched Bud. She shook her shoulders and closed her eyes. Her mouth hung open and her dark teeth showed. She is proud of having her own teeth, no matter how they look. I was glad I had not told her that Mr. Grask kissed me the last afternoon when I went to his room to tell him goodbye. I suppose I will tell her some day, but I'm glad I haven't yet.

"Maybe I'm a witch. Maybe I read minds," my grandmother chuckled. She sounded as if she really had read my mind, but I did not turn my head, and I wasn't angry any more, all of a sudden.

"He was my English teacher," I said to Bud's profile. "I've just started telling Grandmother about him. I'd rather you didn't say anything at home, if you please, Bud, not that you would, of course." I sounded very ladylike and mature to make up for Grandmother.

I wish Grandmother hadn't spoken up, because it would have been interesting to see what Bud would have answered, if anything. My grandmother said, "We're all in love; nobody's making fun, baby." She punched me again, and she said, "I accepted the idea of love a long time ago, and that's the truth." She sounded rather obscene, but I remembered how nice she had been about Mr. Grask, and I said "Of course," or something similar.

We were in sight of town, with the water tower and the steeple of the Presbyterian church, and I wanted to say, "Hurry, hurry." I even thought the way you will think foolish things, that maybe I would reach over and press my foot on the accelerator until the needle swam to seventy, and we would be stopping in front of home. Bud stretched his lips, and his teeth showed white as blossoms. That is a habit of Bud's. He does it before he speaks, as if he had to warm up his mouth to talk. Grandmother always says Bud keeps his counsel better than any of us which may be true.

Bud said, "What do you think about me bringing somebody to live with me?"

My grandmother didn't seem to hear him, and Bud stretched his lips and asked the question again. The speedometer fish went down to ten.

"Male or female?" my grandmother said. She straightened herself, and she stopped playing a crazy old woman with dark teeth.

"Female," Bud said.

My grandmother cleared her throat. I don't know whether she

meant what she said, but she sounded very ladylike. "I've always thought it would be good for you to be married, Bud." Then she said, "You're forty-three years old."

I said, "I think that would be very nice."

Grandmother said, "Who is she?"

Bud said, "She don't live around here. You don't know her." He turned his face to us. It was rather shocking because Bud generally doesn't look straight at you. He said, "She's a mighty good cook."

My grandmother spoke up quickly. "The kitchen is not my province, you know that."

Bud said, "I didn't figure you'd let Miss Dorothy move the kitchen."

"It's not your province either." My grandmother wet her lips, and she said, "I will consider speaking to Dorothy Elizabeth about your wife," and we were at home.

Bud got out and helped us out of the car, which he generally doesn't do. He touched my arm with his hand which is very strong; I said, "Thank you," and my grandmother didn't say anything. We walked up the steps and that was the end of the drive.

Now that I have written it out, the drive does not seem very important since the only new things in it were mentioning Mr. Grask and Bud's wife, which I do not very much believe will happen. Perhaps I should try to write out carefully what happened during dinner, but even though it was interesting I am not really so interested in it as in the afternoon. The rest of the evening reminds me of coming home from an ordinary drive when you have already seen everything once and the fences and the fields have already happened. This does not sound as clear as I would like for it to, but it is hard to be accurate in figures of speech as Mr. Grask was always pointing out.

Dr. Thaxton was at our house for dinner which is not unusual, since his wife has been away visiting for six months at least. The unusual thing is that he had another doctor with him from Louisville. The other doctor and Dr. Thaxton asked my grandmother a good many questions. Every so often my father would break in and tell a little story about Miami or some place, but my mother would turn to Dr. Thaxton and tell him to go ahead. The word *love*, incidentally, was used several times in different ways, but I was not very attentive to the conversation. Just before dessert my grandmother stood up and told my mother to tell Bud to get the car. My mother raised her eyebrows and said, "See?" to the other doctor. She told grandmother to sit down and not be upset, making my grandmother sound somewhat out of her mind. My father said, "Dorothy, if I were you . . ." and my grandmother said, "It's quite perfectly all right," and she went out the terrace door and called Bud and he answered right away. Then we heard the car start. My mother was sitting there frozen, and when the car sounded she pressed her napkin against her lips and said, "My God." Dr. Thaxton jumped up then and patted her shoulder, and my mother put her hand over his.

Everything happened too quickly to think about. The other doctor was excusing himself, and mother said, "We have to do something, we have to." Dr. Thaxton said, "We will, I promise you," and my father said, "Alice and I will have our dessert in the living room."

"You're not coming with us?" my mother said to him.

My father smiled and he said, "I am not."

"If we hurry," Dr. Thaxton said.

My mother looked at us and she said, "Very well," to Dr. Thaxton. He was pulling back her chair when my father and I went into the parlor.

My father turned on the record player, and I guess perhaps I started to cry a little. He said, "We will not talk about anything concerning our family." He smiled very brightly and he said I could write it all out later if I wanted to. He said, "It is very nice to be the father of a creative writer." Then he began to tell stories about horses and other friends of his. You could say my father glitters when he talks. At ten o'clock he said we should have a glass of wine together, which he has never said before. He filled mine partly with water, and I enjoyed it.

I suppose I should be very worried and sleepless about everything, but I am not. I am pretty sure the other ladies in our family will get in before too long, and I imagine we will all go back to being the way we were, almost, anyhow. The word *love* is very interesting to think about, but I am not sad in the least.

The Terrible Death of Mister Vimont

When Beth Dutton turned the car off Main Street onto Sycamore, she was not thinking about Mrs. Vimont at all. She would admit, oh indeed, she would be the first to admit if a policeman, for instance, had asked her, that she thought about Mrs. Vimont almost all the time; but no policeman would ever come poking around, and Mrs. Vimont would keep on living in her little house with the fence around it, and everybody would keep on saying she was a perfect lady. They would say Beth was a lady, too. A person couldn't be around Mrs. Vimont for long without being a perfect lady.

Shortly after Mrs. Vimont had moved up the street, George said that Beth thought more of her than she did of him. It was summer then. They were sitting at the kitchen table. "It's one of your jokes," Beth said. She couldn't look at George, so she looked out the window at the children in the back yard. "It's a joke like 'Is it hot enough for you?'—like you're always saying to the depositors."

George laughed his whinny laugh. "You're O.K., Beth, and Mrs. Vimont's a mighty nice lady."

"George." She made herself look at him. "George, I feel real close to her."

His Adam's apple jerked in his thin neck. He nodded as if he were the president of the bank instead of only just the third teller. "You got to build up the customers' ego. It's psychology, honey," George said, and she didn't talk about Mrs. Vimont any more.

But she thought about her, almost all the time, even when she was with Kelly. Mrs. Vimont was such a lady that you didn't want her to know you smoked, even, or occasionally, ever so occasionally, took little sips from the bottle which George kept hid under the sink, behind the Tide box, so Little George wouldn't be asking a lot of dumb questions. When Mrs. Vimont came to stay with the children, a person couldn't keep from cleaning all the ashtrays and checking twice to make sure the big yellow and orange box really did hide the bottle. Beth always gargled, too, just in case Mrs. Vimont should think for one minute that Beth Dutton wasn't a perfect lady.

Yet, at five o'clock (the courthouse clock had just struck), Thursday, George's afternoon off, September seventeenth, she was not thinking about Mrs. Vimont; and, suddenly, there she was, going into Roberts' Drug Store by the Sycamore Street entrance, the glass door closing behind her.

Mrs. Vimont wore a violet and black checked suit.

Beth pulled the car to the curb; she turned off the ignition key. She reached over and took a road map from the glove compartment and fanned at her face, even though the day was cool for September, just good suit weather she had told herself when she left the house. Her arm, whose hand held the map with the road to Owensboro marked in ink because they had visited George's family again, was covered with violet and black checks.

She looked down at the new suit, mussed now because Kelly was always so excited and hurried about everything. It was not fair for Mrs. Vimont to go out and buy a suit like hers; it was like sneaking up on a person when she wasn't looking; it took a person's breath. If anyone were in the back seat of the car, George, for instance, he would have heard her breathing.

She lowered the road map to the floor of the car, carefully so that it wouldn't rattle; then, she lifted the map and replaced it in the glove compartment. She didn't want George asking questions, not even little questions like, "What's this map doing on the floor?" She closed the door so silently that she could not hear the click herself.

But, of course, George was not in the back seat, as she knew well before she looked. He was at home with Little George and Carole Anne, and she knew it very well. He was riding the children on his thin shoulders, making a fool of himself so the children would be crazy about him. Carole Anne would have mussed up his hair and the bald spot would be showing as white as anything. "Ride, horsie; ride, horsie, ride," he would sing and trot from the living room to the kitchen and back again.

Beth laughed aloud in the quiet car; that is, she started to laugh aloud—she stopped herself just in time so that it sounded like a sneeze. If Mrs. Vimont were standing at Beth's elbow—both in their violet and black checked suits—she would have thought it was a sneeze. But the suits proved only that Mrs. Vimont admired Beth Dutton's taste; she must have just bought the suit—as a surprise for Beth Dutton. They belonged to one person. They could laugh aloud in the darkening street.

Beth placed her foot on the starter. "Keep this minute," she prayed to someone, probably Mrs. Vimont. Her body hummed like the motor, and the tune the radio had been playing in Kelly's room. (Poor George had never noticed how much better the car was running since Kelly had gone over it. Poor Kelly.) When she thought of Kelly's trying to hum *The Blue Danube* along with the radio, she had to laugh again. His thick dark hair fell over his forehead; he looked down at her with his deep, dark eyes; but he had missed the tune entirely. She was so happy that she wanted to shout the words which Kelly shouted, but she only whispered them to herself. The words were funny in Mrs. Vimont's body which had just left Kelly who couldn't carry a tune even with the portable radio close against the bed. "Keep this minute."

The very first time she looked into Mrs. Vimont's eyes, she had felt the union, a drained quiet peace, like religion, as if the blood in her body had flowed to meet the blood of fat little Mrs. Vimont, whose hair was as white as lamb's wool. It was a cold spring morning.

Beth Dutton had stood at the sink, moving a dishmop over a

plate time and time again. She tried to close her mind to the children and to George and to the days which limped after each other like a parade of cripples.

"Walk. Go. By by. Walk. Go," Carole Anne said over and over.

"She wants to take a walk," Little George shouted. "Can't you hear her?"

Beth yanked the rubber gloves from her hands and threw the mop into the water; soap and grease splashed onto her housecoat and onto the floor.

"All right, all right. We'll walk." She turned on Little George, hating his running nose and his scuffed shoes. "Hell, yes, we'll walk." And the dirty diapers would pile up and she would never get the house cleaned, and it would be time to go after Big George. "How's my little family?" he would say.

"Walk. Go. By by," Carole Anne said.

Little George ran his dirty hand down the side of his face, leaving the paths of his fingers on his cheek. Beth was sorry that he looked so much like Big George. She stopped and put her arms around him. "Kiss Mother." She nuzzled against his neck. Little George did not move. "Kiss Mother," she said. "Kiss me."

He turned his face to hers, but he did not move his lips. She pretended that he had kissed her. She said, "That's Mother's boy." Her head ached. She did not like to quarrel with the children.

But she had a terrible time getting them into their coats. The lining of Carole Anne's sleeve was loose and she kept digging her hand in the wrong place and crying about it, enough to drive a person crazy. "Broke. Broke, Mamma," Carole Anne said over and over, while George swung the front door back and forth and called, "Come on. Hurry up. What's the matter with you?"

Outside it was as cold as winter. Daffodils and hyacinths looked crazy waving in the wind. The sky was close against the naked trees.

Carole Anne lifted her legs stiffly; she threw her stomach out; she staggered from one side of the walk to the other. "Walk straight," Beth Dutton said to her daughter, but to herself she spoke her own name with fear. Beth Rice, who owned three silver cups to tell that she was beautiful, was the wife of George Dutton, teller. Beth Rice Dutton.

"Little George. Come back. Walk with us," she called without expecting him to pay any attention to her.

George held out his arms. "I'm a jet." He tore down the sidewalk towards them. "Look out, you."

Carole Anne began to scream before George knocked her down. Beth grabbed at George's arm. She made her voice low; it was difficult to speak through the lump of anger that pressed against her throat. "George," she said. "George, listen to me." She pinched his arm, hoping that he could feel pain through his leather jacket. "Just you wait till we get home, young man."

He tried to pull away from her. Carole Anne began to laugh. "George, please," Beth said. "Please."

"Dord, Dord," Carole Anne said.

"I brought you a present." George took the head of a jonquil from his jacket pocket. He held the head towards her, white against his dirty hands.

"What have I told you about other people's property?"

"It's a present. The fat lady that moved in the house . . ."

Beth snatched the flower and closed her hand over it. She pressed her nails into the petals. She trembled in the cold spring day. "Haven't I told you a thousand times? Over and over I've told you."

"I didn't pick it." George stuck out his mouth. He looked more than ever like his father.

"Don't lie to me." It was hard to whisper.

"She did. She told me to pick it. She really really did." George's eyes were bright and smart-aleck.

"We won't talk about it any more." She gritted her teeth until they hurt.

"She did tell me. The new lady on the corner. She told me."

Beth jabbed the torn flower into George's pocket. "Now leave it there—forever. And get away from me. Don't let me hear another word out of you."

George reached out and pushed Carole Anne. He ran up the street yelling, "You can't catch me."

"Get up, Carole Anne. You're not a bit hurt."

"Dord broke Carole."

"Come on. Get up."

Beth closed her eyes. She staggered on the walk, like Carole Anne. "Lord God. Dord God." She wished she could sleep a long time, until Carole Anne was toilet-trained and George was rid of his cold, until the children were in school and able to dress themselves and go to bed without being yelled at, until Big George was dead and it was always June.

She had not known that the woman was crouched by the fence. Beth opened her eyes, and suddenly, as if in a dream, the woman rose beside her. Beth called out—"Lord," or, "Oh," or something —she would never remember what she called out. In front of her, on the slope of the yard, a white-haired lady, round and smiling, lifted her fat white hand to adjust the glasses on her nose. "I didn't mean to frighten you," the woman said.

Beth could not speak for a minute. She could not remember ever having faced another human being whose eyes were on exactly the same level, to the thousandth of an inch. It was like looking into a mirror.

"My name is Mrs. Vimont," the woman said. "I'm your neighbor." The woman's voice was low and pretty. She smiled. "You'll come in and have a cup of coffee, won't you? And milk, milk for the children."

"I'm sorry. You scared me." Beth's voice was quiet, like the woman's.

They both turned to watch George. Beth wished he wouldn't make such a fool of himself; he yelled and put one foot in the street and drew it back and yelled again. She started to say, "I wish he wouldn't make such a fool of himself."

"He's a fine boy," the woman said.

"About the jonquil," Beth heard herself say to the steady blue eyes in front of her.

"I told him to take it." The woman's eyes misted suddenly. She looked down at Carole Anne. "You are fortunate to have two such beautiful children."

Beth reached for Carole Anne's hand. "George."

He came running towards her. "I didn't do anything."

"Honey, we're going in to see Mrs. Vimont."

George and Carole Anne sat cross-legged on the fender. They played quietly with a box of buttons, smiling at each other like children in a photograph. Beth Dutton sat on the flowered cretonne couch beside the mahogany table which held the green pottery vase of blue hyacinths. Mrs. Vimont's voice, like water, smoothed and rippled over the room. Beth felt her own blood move warm and quiet. For only a moment she thought of Big George and his baths: the green electric heater on the laundry hamper pulled close against the tub, the room hot as a steam cabinet; George, laughing, his skinny body covered with soap, blinking his eyes at the children who insisted on watching Daddy bathe.

"Your house is so pretty." Beth sat taller. "It's a funny thing—you pass a house every day, going to the grocery or downtown, and you don't see what you pass, really see it, I mean."

"That's very true, dear." Mrs. Vimont smiled. She rested her hand on Beth's arm. "I hadn't thought about it."

Beth was afraid she was going to cry. "I hadn't thought about it either. But I'll never pass your house again without seeing it as hard as I can."

"What a sweet thing to say." Mrs. Vimont patted Beth.

"And you know what? I . . . I feel as if something wonderful was about to happen. Just meeting you." She was surprised at her words. It was as if Mrs. Vimont had told her the words to say.

"Dear, how nice. And I know what you're talking about. I feel it, too."

Suddenly they were telling each other of all the days which had gone before this day. It was like being young and on a date with a brand-new person you liked very much, and you felt you had to catch up on everything, and maybe this person was the person you were going to live happily ever after with. It had been that way with George at Atlantic City that first night. Beth thought of George for only a moment. The George she told Mrs. Vimont about was a little different from the other George, but he was almost the same.

Mrs. Vimont said, "Poor dear." And she said, "It's so difficult when one's in-laws try to live your life for you," and she clucked her tongue.

Beth said, "We've been here almost a year now. It's a lonely town."

"It's sad, so sad for you," Mrs. Vimont said.

"But George's father just made us come here. At the bank, he had a whole lot of . . . influence," she had almost said *pull*, "and they bought us this house on a street where there weren't any other children, and—they've been awfully sweet, of course, buying us things, but . . ."

"I know, I know," Mrs. Vimont said, and her eyes misted.

Perhaps, Beth thought, the tears which did not fall from the old lady's eyes made the color such a bright clean blue.

The tears did not fall even when Mrs. Vimont told of Eloise who had died the night of her eighth-grade graduation. "I think she would have been as beautiful as you," Mrs. Vimont said. Her voice was softly steady, even when she spoke of Mr. Vimont who, last winter, in the big snow, had started for the neighborhood drugstore. "He stepped on a live wire. He was electrocuted," Mrs. Vimont said, "terribly." Beth could not keep from crying.

"I knew I couldn't live in Pittsburgh any more, not ever again. And so I came here, where my Mamma lived when she was a little girl. She used to talk about it a great deal. I bought this house, sight unseen, and then this morning you walked down the street."

Little George sitting on the fender, a milk mustache almost to his nose, seemed to understand the sympathy which moved in the room. He said, "Mrs. Beemont, your eyes are just like Mamma's, only you're fatter."

"George," Beth said, pretending to be embarrassed, but loving George very much.

Mrs. Vimont laughed and tousled George's hair. "We are good friends, all of us—George, and Carole Anne, and Mamma, and I."

That very afternoon Mrs. Vimont asked to keep the children. "You will let me, won't you? It's not often a person has the good fortune to sit with the children of a beauty queen. Go to a movie or something; just get out for a little while."

"Really. Really?" Beth said.

She had honestly planned to go to a movie, but as she passed the new service station which had opened on the corner of Main and Broadway, she noticed that the car—it had been a present from George's parents—was almost out of gas. She felt giddy, almost drunk, as she pulled under the dancing pennants and the twirling metal streamers. "I'm fortunate. I'm a fortunate girl," she said aloud. The tall handsome man whom she had glanced at yesterday as she took George back to the bank stood beside the car. "How long will it take to change the oil?" she asked.

The man nodded to one of the square-faced boys who leaned against the gleaming white wall of the station. "Hey, Ed." The man looked at her deeply, clear through her. There had been no time to think. "It'll take the boy about thirty minutes on that oil," he said, and she had followed him into the room behind the station, without even knowing his name. "Next time we'll go to a motel. We'll do it up right next time."

At first they had met only once a week, on Monday because George was always late coming home on Monday. Then they had added Friday, and, after a little while, by the middle of summer, there was no schedule. Kelly would call her at home, and she would say, "A minute, just a minute," and, as often as not, Mrs. Vimont would scratch at the door, sensing that Beth Dutton wanted to run downtown for a little while. Of course, on Thursdays, George, blinking and bald as a man in a cartoon, insisted on staying with the children. It was hard to tell which was the best day of the week.

In four months the world had changed: Little George and Carole Anne and the housework and even Big George, who was rather sweet, though he often sat and looked at her without speaking, and once in a while he mentioned going back to Owensboro to live. "I've told you. I've told you I won't ever go there again, George," she said quietly, and he turned from her, reaching for the paper, or winding his watch, or retying the laces of his polished shoes. She watched his awkward movements with a kind of pity—she guessed it was pity—and sometimes she reached over and kissed his head. She almost wished, sometimes, that George could find a Mrs. Vimont for himself. "You only live once," Beth said. Mrs. Vimont had said the same thing. "A person only lives once," Mrs. Vimont said, "so I just decided to go on and buy the azalea-mums and enjoy them, even though they were ever so dear." Anybody else would have said *expensive*. Beth told Kelly about the azalea-mums. "She's the sweetest lady in the world," she told Kelly, and Kelly said, "Sure, sure she is," and pulled her down to him again, laughing in his throat.

It was hard to remember time before Mrs. Vimont. Together they sewed for the children, and worked in Mrs. Vimont's garden, and canned tomatoes and green beans, never once getting in each other's way. After silence, they spoke the same words, "I forgot to tell you," or, "Did you see in the paper?" or, "Yesterday, I . . ." Always with Mrs. Vimont, with Kelly—it was hard to keep them really separate in her mind, there was the same complete union of meeting for the first time.

"Honestly, we're just like twins," Mrs. Vimont said.

"It's true, it's true," Beth said. And it was true. Sometimes, of course, she had made up little similarities to please the old lady—like loving Strauss waltzes or the color violet, but as soon as she made them up they were very true. She honestly adored Strauss waltzes, though Kelly could never carry the tune. There was no color in the world like violet. Mrs. Vimont said so, and Beth felt very close to all of Mrs. Vimont's life: her mother, and her friends, and the houses she had lived in, and the clothes she had worn, and, naturally, Mr. Vimont. Sometimes, alone, Beth cried because Mr. Vimont had lain in the snow until the taxi driver found him. She sat at her dressing table and said, "Poor, poor Mr. Vimont."

In the eyes of her mind she could see him, just as she could see George and Kelly, the skin on their knuckles, and the pattern of their mouths, and the line of their hair. Seeing them made it even stranger that alone, away from Mrs. Vimont, she had never been able to experience her presence, even though she had worked very hard at it, holding a snapshot in her hand and trying to force the picture to bring Mrs. Vimont into the room. Several times she had slammed the snapshot on the dressing table and run from the house, no matter if the children were crying, to bathe, if only for a few minutes, in the quiet peace of the little old lady to whom life had already happened. She had thought that the magic lay in Mrs. Vimont's eyes. Yet, she must have known, deep inside her bones, that some day she would be able to feel the union, even when Mrs. Vimont stood before a glass counter in Roberts' Drug Store and Beth Dutton pulled her car to a stop in front of her own house, eleven blocks away.

She stopped the motor, and the presence did not leave her. She opened and closed the car door, and still she felt the clean pull of Mrs. Vimont's eyes, of her own eyes which were Mrs. Vimont's. She bathed in Mrs. Vimont's cleanness which was her own, covered with a suit of violet and black checks.

Behind the glass of the front window stood George with Carole Anne on his shoulders. Little George beat upon the glass, leaving the marks of his fingers. George's bald spot showed very white where Carole Anne had mussed his hair.

"Hello," she called. "Hello." It was hard to keep from laughing aloud, but George would ask silly questions which would make her angry, and she did not want to be angry. When she was in the house she said, "How's everybody?" but, of course, George didn't notice that the voice belonged to Mrs. Vimont.

"Fine. Fine." George swung Carole Anne to the floor. "Whee," he said.

"What'd you buy? Did you bring us anything?"

"Bring Carole thing."

She kneeled and let Little George and Carole Anne kiss her on either cheek. "Darlings," she said. "Not a thing, I couldn't find a thing you'd like. Next time, though, I will. I promise."

Carole Anne looked as if she were going to cry. "Now, Carole Anne. I told you there wasn't anything. I've told you." She stood, although it was really difficult to rise from a kneeling position, and patted George's arm. "Did you get along all right?"

"Fine. Fine as frog's hair." George took a cigarette and a paper of matches from his shirt pocket. Beth watched him without speaking. He closed the cover of the match folder before he struck the match. He smiled at her. "Good weather, isn't it? Nice and cool."

"Fine," she said, and looked away. "You very hungry?"

"We had cookies," Little George said. "Daddy bought us cookies."

"Cookies," Carole Anne said.

"Look, George, we'll eat after the children do. You'll have plenty of time for your bath." She moved past him into the bedroom to leave her hat and gloves on the dressing table which held the three silver trophies gleaming strangely in the dusk. She did not light the lamps. "I won't be a minute," she called. "I won't even change my clothes." She did not look straight into the mirror above the dressing table, but sideways, the way an actress would look into a camera. She ran her hands deep into the pockets of her suit coat, and waited a moment before the mirror. She could not see her face, but she knew she was beautiful.

In the bathroom George started filling the tub. "See anybody in town?" he yelled.

Beth closed her eyes. She did not want to be angry. George knew very well that he couldn't hear above the sound of the water, yet he always tried to carry on a conversation while he undressed. "Hunh? Hunh? Talk louder. What you say?"

Beth swung open the bathroom door. "No. Not a soul," she said. Already steam filled the room, like perspiration. Already the electric heater was on the laundry hamper pulled close against the tub.

"Hey, you're exposing me," George said, pretending to cover himself.

"I'm sorry," Beth said. "I can't make myself heard above the water."

"Sure, I keep forgetting." George smiled slyly. "How about a kiss for your old man?"

"George!"

"Watch Daddy," Carole Anne said at the door.

"We're going to help Daddy take his bath."

"We'll do nothing of the kind," Beth said. "Daddy deserves some privacy. You come with me. I won't be a minute."

"It's O.K., Bethie," George said.

"No, really. Their supper's almost ready."

Little George began to whine, but she took his arm and led him from the bathroom. Carole Anne followed. "Carole help Daddy," she said.

"Peanut butter sandwiches," Beth said. "How will that be?"

Her hands moved separate from her mind, drowning the sound of the children's voices. Her hands moved very quickly. It was a pleasure to watch them. They smoothed a clean white cloth on the kitchen table, though the children were death on clean cloths; they fixed cocoa, and spread peanut butter on soft white bread.

"Up we go." Beth lifted Carole Anne to her highchair. "Sit down, George boy. That's a fellow."

In the bathroom the water stopped.

Beth removed her apron and placed the rubber gloves on her swift hands. She smoothed the fingers as carefully as if she were dressing for a party. A person couldn't be too careful. Mrs. Vimont said so. Kelly said so, too. "Wait a minute. You can't be too careful," Kelly always said.

"Now," Beth said. "You have plenty to eat?"

"More," Carole Anne said.

"Really, Carole Anne," Beth said, but she poured each of the children an extra mug of cocoa. "There, two cups apiece, and you aren't to move until you've finished every single drop. You'll see that Carole Anne finishes every single drop, won't you, George boy?"

"I can boss Carole Anne."

"Every single drop. Now remember."

Big George lay back in the tub. He turned his thin ugly face towards her, squinting his eyes. In her violet and black checked suit she stood close against the tub and looked down at George's body covered with soap.

"Hello, beautiful," he said.

She did not answer. She did not have to use her hands, but she was glad she had worn the gloves. She crouched, the toe of her left foot braced against the side of the tub, and swung her hip against the heater. "Mister Vimont," she said. "Mister Vimont."

George's mouth was shaped like a zero. He might have been going to say, "Oh, Beth, you can't guess what Carole Anne did this afternoon," or, "Oh, did I tell you who came in the bank this morning and asked especially for me?" or "Oh, Beth, you are a beautiful woman."

She closed the door carefully, and tiptoed into the bedroom.

"I'm finished," Little George called, but she did not answer him.

In a little while she would discover Big George. She would go to the telephone by the bed and call Mrs. Vimont whose husband lay dead and buried. "It's wonderful to be alive, isn't it wonderful?" Mrs. Vimont always said, and she was really quite a woman. It was all a big joke that made you want to laugh in the dark house, the house was very dark—everybody thinking she was such a perfect lady. Beth hoped the little old perfect lady had bought the violet and black checked suit on sale. Mr. Vimont wasn't such a good provider, not the way George had been. She hadn't given it much thought before, but she was proud of George. It made everything so much funnier.

She looked straight into the mirror so that she could get the full view of herself. She could see without any light. It was a big joke, as if the suit had stretched to Mrs. Vimont's size. It was all you could do to keep from laughing. She moved, almost stealthily—Mrs. Vimont loved the word *stealthily*—closer and closer to the mirror. She leaned far over the dressing table until the silver cups pressed against her breasts. She parted her lips, as if she were about to be kissed, and then she pulled back, steadying the cups with her hands. She sat on the dressing table stool and waited.

"We're through. It's dark," Little George called. "I bossed Carole Anne."

"Boss George," Carole Anne said.

Beth ran her tongue over her lips. "Stay there. Wait till I come." But she heard the scrape of Little George's chair and the sound of his feet, and his voice saying, "Where are you? Where are you, Mamma?"

She closed her eyes and turned her head, her chin pressed so tightly against the cloth of her suit that she could feel the checks. "Here I am, George boy. I'm here in the bedroom."

Beside her in the dark room Little George began to cry. "I want my Mamma. Please, I want my Mamma."

She struck him full in the mouth. He backed away from her until he was against the telephone table. His eyes were white.

"Move. Move, George," she said. She dialed Mrs. Vimont without thinking of the numbers.

"Hello," Mrs. Vimont said. "Hello."

Beth held the receiver away from her and let George's sobs wash against the mouthpiece.

Later she would call Kelly. She raised her hand to her mouth. She did not want to cry yet. But, suddenly, she could not remember Kelly at all, his face, or his body, or the feel of his hands.

"Mrs. Vimont," she cried. "Oh, Mrs. Vimont."

Cafe Nore

I suppose everyone has heard of the Cafe Nore. If you go to the Cafe you'll always see someone you know, people say. And you're bound to go sooner or later, they say, and you'll never forget the entertainment. Perhaps everything they say is true, but I am not sure. Perhaps the Cafe is not inevitable.

I am sure Ellen and I never planned to go, yet I suppose we had always planned to—the way we were and were not going to Paris or the South Seas or the moon. A pediatrician's life is pretty pleasantly cut out for him; unless there is a medical convention in Paris or the moon, he's not very likely to get there. The habit of making a convention a vacation is as ingrained in a doctor's life as, say, the habit of making money. I write as honestly as I can. Ellen and I did not speak of the Cafe any more than we spoke of her young men, or religion, or death. Now that she has gone—now that she has died by her own hand (as they say), I feel it is important to record all I remember of the Cafe Nore, of which we did not speak.

It was in winter that we went. We had not been looking for it. We had been at the Thompsons' for one of those parties which doctors regularly give for each other—Thompson is a surgeon; there was the carefully detailed dinner, punctuated by first one of us then another's crumpling his napkin to answer the telephone, to return to the table smiling; the hurried drinking with the men gathered at the far end of the room, the women talking in flamingo voices around the coffee table; the strong black coffee at eleven. Ellen had another drink instead of coffee, but I didn't worry. One rarely has time for too much alcohol at a Thompson dinner. "I have an operation at seven," the men said. The women spoke of sitters. And we were going down the steps, husbands and wives clinging to each other. As usual we called "Goodnight, goodnight." I was conscious of Ellen's breath and my breath hanging cold before us as we called. I was also conscious of the immensity of the words, and I was annoyed at my consciousness. While I never refer to myself as a man of science, as do so many of my compatriots, I am generally not sentimental. I thought I had learned to accept the world as I have accepted war and injury.

When we were in the car, Ellen slid across the slick seat covers to sit very close beside me. Her perfume was heavy. I wondered if she had put it on while I was going around to my side of the car, while I paused to call "So long" again to the Thompsons who waved behind their shining storm door. I smelled the cold and the newness of the car and Ellen's perfume.

"So long," Ellen said softly.

I was extremely uncomfortable when she said, "It's a very brave and unselfish thing to say. 'So long' is, I mean, brave to say." I cannot remember her having said such a thing in the years of our marriage.

I said, "The Thompsons are pleasant people."

She said, "I'm glad you're nothing but a phony doctor. I'm glad you don't operate every morning at seven, and I'm glad we don't have to hurry home for a sitter." Then she was crying.

I said, "Please, Ellen," although I had grown accustomed to her sudden tears, and I was not unsympathetic. Always her tears were quiet and brief, and I had long ago accepted the nature of my profession. We never mentioned her crying, any more than we mentioned the Cafe.

"The miracle drugs aren't any miracle, are they?" She pressed her handkerchief against her mouth. Her eyes were very large in the red light.

I said, "You don't get enough rest. You need a change."

"From red to yellow to green," she said as I pressed my foot against the accelerator. She laughed swiftly. She leaned against my shoulder. "I'm all right. I just need to get crazy about something, I guess. I don't really mind not having children. I've never told you I don't mind, have I? I'm glad, really. I'll get interested in something or somebody. You're not to worry. I wouldn't have a husband who was a father, too. I mean that."

"You're interested in too much—too many things," I said. "You could take a little trip now. And we'll be going to New York in the spring. You could fly to Bermuda, for instance."

"Or Paris or the moon." She sat very straight.

Instead of turning right off Main, I had headed for the old Richmond Road. Ellen used to enjoy aimless driving. When we were young, when I first came back home to practice, we often drove around in the evening. Ellen had been particularly fond of the old Richmond Road. For all I knew she still drove it with her young men—the eager young internes and the others.

"Or I could go to the Cafe Noir. *We* could, Harold. We're always hearing about it, aren't we? Haven't you always heard of the Cafe Noir?"

"I don't even have any idea what it is." I laughed as heartily as I could. "It's probably just a myth—like the moment of decision which comes once to every child and boy and man." I expected her to laugh.

"Or woman. I want to go. To the Cafe Noir, the Cafe Noir, the Cafe Noir." She called the name, as if she were a child making a wish.

"Je ne sais pas," I said.

"Noir, noir." Ellen giggled suddenly. "Quoth the raven, 'ever noir.' "

I put my arm around Ellen. I felt young, as if I were happy. I said, "J'adore noir."

"It isn't *noir* at all. But it's just as good. Look, Harold!" There was no memory of tears in her voice. "It's every bit as good. Ever *Nore*. I adore *Nore*."

If she had not called I would have missed the discreet yellow sign which flashed for a moment in the car lights at the curve beyond the Elkhorn bridge.

The two words written in white were placed beneath each other, as neatly as an inscription on stone:

Cafe
Nore

"That's it?" The young-man feeling, the brief moment of drunken affection and unity, was gone.

"It has to be. Back up in a hurry, Harold. To think we almost missed it, and I've been out this road hundreds of times. Just to think, Harold!"

A graveled drive, only wide enough for one car, led up to the old house. To the right of the house was a vast concrete parking lot lit by a single electric bulb high on a pole in the very center of the area. I pressed the button to lower my window. In the cold air I thought that the light wavered under water, as if Ellen and I moved through a gray world of rocks and fish.

Ellen did not wait for me to open the door for her. She stood against the light pole, hugging her handsome fur coat around herself, calling, "Hurry, Harold. For heaven's sake, hurry."

Her voice was very loud. I did not want to discourage her sudden good humor, but I did not like the way she was calling the attention of the cold night to ourselves. I didn't even take time to lock the car.

"Careful, you'll scare the fish," I said when I reached her.

But she spoke more loudly than ever, leaning heavily against me as we began to follow the broad white stripe on the concrete. "Our car's the nicest car here," she shouted. "Look, Harold!"

"Yes, of course," I whispered. There were perhaps twenty cars hunched in the gray light. Most of them were old models, with crunched fenders and broken glass. "Yes, Ellen."

The painted stripe curved down an incline. It ended with a painted arrow. Before us rose the entrance walk, mounting in waves to the Cafe Nore. The house was like any old house, built a long time ago, back from the Richmond Road. Perhaps that is the reason Ellen and I, or Ellen and her young men, had never noticed it before. Perhaps it was like any old house—square and brick—except there were no trees, and instead of a sloping lawn there was only concrete stretching on either side of the walk.

"It's like any old house on the road, isn't it, Harold?" Ellen shouted. "Isn't it, Harold?"

"Yes. Yes, Ellen."

"It looks like that picture in the Modern Museum, something like it. You know, the house by the railroad. Maybe that's the name of it, 'The House by the Railroad.' "

"There isn't any railroad out here," I said.

"But it does look like it. It does, Harold." She sounded disappointed, as if she might cry again.

"Of course it does." I could not remember the picture.

The three stone steps to the porch were as worn as if the concrete waves of the yard had washed over them since time. Ellen stumbled.

"I don't think I want to go," she said slowly. But the beveled glass door was opening, as if by an electric eye, and I am sure it was Ellen who moved first toward the door.

In a wide hall, beneath a hanging light covered with a pumpkin yellow shade fringed with beads, a girl in a gypsy costume said, "Check your coats."

Ellen looked at me over her shoulder. Her face was not smiling, but it was not sad, either. In the yellow light she looked very young, almost as young as the girl who extended her white arms for my coat and hat.

"No," Ellen said, nestling her hands beneath the collar of her coat, pressing the collar tabs against her cheeks.

Although I knew that the gypsy girl was speaking a cliche, for a moment I could not understand her words. "You won't feel it when you go out," she said again. I listened very carefully. She rubbed the tips of her fingers over my hat and smiled.

"Hurry," Ellen said. "This is like a date, isn't it? This is like slumming and being ever so young all over."

I thought of kissing the gypsy girl's young mouth. It had been a very long time since I had felt like kissing a stranger's mouth. Her lips were pursed, as if she said, "Urgent," or, "Soon, soon." I said the words in my mind. Of course I did not kiss her.

Ellen kept smiling at me over her shoulder, the way a woman smiles in an advertisement for jewels or depilatories. I followed her to an empty table, where a man in a scarlet coat pulled back our chairs. I am sure Ellen did not pay any attention to the man. If she had noticed him, I would remember his face, the way I remember the other faces—the internes, and the man at the supermarket and the riding instructor. But in the Cafe Nore, Ellen did not smile at the young man.

"Nore," Ellen's mouth said. "It can't mean anything. Nore." She pressed her lips together.

But it was difficult to adjust my eyes to the candlelight of the Cafe. I removed my glasses and wiped them with my handkerchief; still it was difficult. Along the heavily curtained walls candles flared in brackets; on our small round table they shone blindingly; above our heads they burned in a great crystal chandelier. At first, I saw nothing but the light.

"It's a terrible fire hazard." Ellen was clutching her coat closer about her, though beads of perspiration stood on her forehead.

I said, "We're a good couple, Ellen. In spite of everything." I was hoping to recall the camaraderie I had felt on the road; naturally, it was impossible.

"It's charming, perfectly charming, Harold," she said, and her lips were as red as blood. Her eyes began to dart around the Cafe. "This must have been the dining room in the old house. And that was the parlor there, beyond the arch. And the people—they look quite like their cars. And look at those funny little grooves running every which way. It's charming, Harold."

Her eyes moved so swiftly that I could not follow them. I concentrated on the series of arches which threw themselves mathematically into the infinity of distance. "There are many rooms," I said.

Ellen's laugh was sharp. "Foolish, foolish, Harold. There are just *two* rooms. You're looking at a mirror. They do it with mirrors—just like in the joke." She began to wave her arms to a figure in the candlelight, and the figure waved back. "There I am. You're there, too, Harold. Wave at us, Harold."

"Not so loud, Ellen," I said before I thought.

Ellen closed her eyes. She laughed helplessly. Her laughter sounded like water pushing itself from a jug. "We saw someone we knew at the Cafe Nore, just the way they said we would."

Behind Ellen's chair stood a waitress. She looked like the girl who had taken my coat. I thought of asking if they were sisters or the same person.

"Will you eat or drink?" the girl asked.

"Drink," I said, remembering the mouth of the first girl.

"Eat," Ellen said, sitting straight again. "You're drunk enough, Harold. A toasted bacon and tomato sandwich and coffee."

The waitress smiled, showing her rather crooked teeth. "It's not the season for tomatoes. We have only things in season."

Ellen was angry. "What the hell is in season?"

"Bourbon, or wine, or . . ."

"A turkey sandwich then, and coffee. Seasonal turkey."

I was sorry Ellen was being difficult about the rules of the Cafe. "Bourbon and water," I said. "If that's all right?"

"They are in season," the girl said. "I'll hurry. It's almost time for the show—the entertainment." When she went away her yellow skirt swung against our table.

Ellen's face was flushed. "I'm not a housewife; I don't fit in the mold," she shouted. "I would be utterly satisfied if you made love to that girl. Don't try to look guilty. Guilt is a great luxury for a fraud, and I refuse to have you reading my mind, I absolutely refuse."

I did not know what she meant, but I was sorry I had forgotten my wife in the presence of the girl. I placed my hand over Ellen's. Beneath the small table our knees touched.

"I'm sure you are capable of making love to her," Ellen said more quietly; and then: "We touch because of the smallness of the table. It's not because of affection, or lust, or even habit. I'm not middle-aged, Harold. You may be, but I'm not."

But she did not shake my hand away.

It was time, I thought, to speak of the subjects we had never discussed.

Ellen said, "Where did we hear of the place? Was it somebody in Boston, or that time in Topeka? Think, Harold. Think. It was at *some* convention. You aren't even trying to think."

"It was in the past." My voice broke, but I was not embarrassed. We can resurrect time together, I thought. I said, "It was since we were married. It was . . ."

But Ellen interrupted; her words ran swiftly after each other. "When I was a child, I was always trying to remember something like this. Who gave me what for Christmas? and where did I see a certain movie? I was forever doing it. I'd get up at night, and try to . . ."

"Us. We," I said. "I'm remembering medical school. You had a cloth coat, and our rooming house in Louisville was very cold at night."

"When I'd lose things I'd go over and over what I'd been doing when I had them last. I'd stand in the center of the room and act it all out. 'I stood here,' I'd say, 'and I opened this drawer.' "

There was movement around us. Ellen turned to watch the curtains being drawn from the walls—the word *drawer* still on her lips.

Because of the vague light and the mirrors it was difficult to tell whether one or a dozen costumed waitresses pulled the curtains. The girls worked so swiftly that their faces blurred. The curtains followed the grooves which made the design of the dark ceiling: they circled, met, and parted like the stitched lines of a quilt. One by one the small tables in the parlor disappeared.

"They'll close us in, too," Ellen said coldly. "Our order hasn't come, either. Stop squinting, Harold."

I was trying to see the faces of the other human beings who waited with us in the Cafe, but I didn't manage. No sooner had I focused my eyes on a table near us than the whirling girl and her curtains enclosed it. In a moment our table, too, was an island.

I held Ellen's hand very tightly. I pressed my knees hard against hers. I said, "I hated every day of those classes—and interning—all of it. I was always afraid I was going to be sick. Then I'd remember I'd be with you in a little while. And I was never sick, because I thought you were waiting for me. I used to come home, to the cold rooming house, and you would . . ."

"Honestly, Harold. This is like Sunday School classes. Did you ever go to Sunday School? Before? Before we were married, Harold?" The bones of Ellen's skeleton pressed against her skin. "We had opening exercises, and then somebody pulled the curtains."

"I used to look at a corpse—which had already passed away—and I'd think, 'This, too, shall pass away.' The war—everything, they did pass away. And I was a doctor with an office."

"The curtains were made of burlap in Sunday School, though. They smelled terrible."

I said, "I thought these were burlap."

"Silly," Ellen said. "Honestly, Harold! They're velvet."

"I wish you wouldn't say 'Honestly, Harold.' We never say honestly."

Ellen moved her hands. "Harold, whatever. Whatever was it happened?" Her eyes, set in her skeleton, were as vacant as the eyes of a fish. For a moment her eyes seemed to swim in the candlelight.

"Whatever," I repeated.

"I loved you," she said. "I know I did. Your—your injury, it wasn't important. I hate children. And besides—we get along all right."

"A person needs to remember, as much as he needs not to remember. We've acted as if it was always now."

"No, no, no, not again. Dear God, not another lecture. I just can't bear to hear you again. 'Maturity is acceptance, acceptance, acceptance.' " Ellen was an effective mimic: her voice sounded very much like my own. Her hands pinched at the faded table cloth as if the cloth were flesh. "But it shouldn't ever be. Nothing should ever be just acceptance."

"But we have details now, here—marriage, and a specific wound," I said. "We don't have the curse of metaphor. This is different, Ellen, with the details here, now."

Ellen said, "We have as good a marriage as any. You talk so much, Harold. You talk and talk and talk."

I looked past her shoulder, but there was no place to look in the curtained enclosure, and our eyes met again. I leaned over the table to kiss her.

She did not seem to be conscious of my lips. Still, we looked at each other until the girl with the yellow skirt stood against our table. I was sorry the girl had appeared.

"How ever did you get in?" Ellen asked. "It must be like trying to find the opening in a stage curtain. Once when I was in high school I came out in front to make a speech or an announcement or something very important and I did it very well, and then I couldn't find where I had come from. I fought the curtains and everyone laughed."

"We have long practice here," the girl said.

"You aren't old enough to have long practice," I said. "At any thing."

The girl said, "They're almost ready for you. They'll be waiting."

"Who's waiting?" Ellen half rose from her chair.

"It's just the entertainment. It's choosing time."

"*Nore* is probably just somebody's last name," Ellen said. She pushed the girl aside; she had no difficulty in finding the curtain's opening. "We're ready. You go ahead and lead the way."

We followed the girl through a labyrinthine aisle. Perhaps we circled the room many times. Ellen spoke loudly. "It's like Halloween. It's like walking Pullman cars that don't end. It's like a burrow. It's like flying on a dark beam. It's like sleep. Talk, Harold. Tell me what it's like, Harold!"

I put my hands on Ellen's shoulders. "It's a curtained aisle, Ellen. It's not like anything."

"Hurry," the girl's voice said ahead of us. "The entertainment."

I had not expected the Minotaur; still I had expected more than another curtained space, only a little larger than the table we had left. Facing us were two curtained stalls, like cabanas. The girl in the yellow skirt and a man in striped trousers were the only attendants. The man was my own height and coloring.

"You'll have to wait a moment," the man said.

"Your coat's awfully pretty," the girl told Ellen.

"Still cold outside?" the man asked.

"It was when we came in," Ellen said, but she did not look at the man. "It's cold enough to bring in your brass monkeys anyhow."

The girl laughed. "I love your coat."

The cabana curtains parted and a man and woman stepped out. Their faces were bright and, I suppose, featureless. I do not know where the light came from—there were no candles. Perhaps there was a ceiling light. I didn't think about the source of light at the time.

"Damn," Ellen said. "I thought it would be somebody we knew."

The man and woman nodded to the attendants and to us. "I don't have words," the man said, before he disappeared with the woman.

"You're next," the waiter said. His voice was confidential.

"You have a bedside manner," Ellen said.

My hands were still on her shoulders. I pushed her toward the cabana the bright-faced woman had vacated. I tried to recall the woman's face. The waitress extended her white arm to pull back the entrance.

Ellen shrugged my hands away. "I'm not going in. I'm just not. Nobody can make me."

"Very well," the girl said. "Just as you like. It's entirely voluntary."

The girl had spoken so calmly that Ellen's voice was quiet when she said, "I'll wait for Harold."

"It's perfectly all right," the girl said. "It's only entertainment."

I was embarrassed by Ellen's attitude, but I had often been embarrassed by her sudden whims and prejudices. At the same time I felt a kind of tenderness. I said, "I wish you'd come."

"Shut up and hurry up," Ellen said, and I walked around her into the cabana.

There was practically nothing to the entertainment of the Cafe. Perhaps my annoyance or my tenderness spoiled the experience—or the cessation of experience—I still do not understand the nature of the entertainment.

There was music and perfume and a sound like wind; in the stall next to me, the one Ellen should have entered, there was a light. As if through net I saw the figure of one of the waitresses. "Choose," she said above the music and the light and the movement of her hands over my body. "Do you choose?"

"Of course," I said, although I did not know what I was choosing.

"You are pretending, aren't you?" the girl asked above my senses which had responded quickly to the stimuli. "It doesn't matter, though. Your way is probably just as good."

For a moment I felt that the curtains were closing in. I was as lightheaded as if I had fainted, the way I fainted when I administered to my first patient after I had become a doctor with an office. I remembered, as drowning men are supposed to remember or create, the day I had fainted in my new office.

"You get your choice," the girl beyond the net said. "It would be nice, though, if you knew what you're choosing."

Her hands lingered for a moment, and that was all. The man in the striped trousers opened the striped doorway. The entertainment had been no more significant than a colored dream.

"But no less significant," the girl said.

"I think I'm going in now," Ellen shouted above the sound of wind. "You wait for me."

But she stopped at the curtained doorway. Perhaps I was relieved to see her stop. When she turned, she looked very chic and composed.

The man in the striped trousers said, "You could have pretended to faint." He was whispering, but the enclosure was so small I could not keep from hearing. "The rules say you can pretend for the entertainment."

"I decided not to go in. I decided against it." Ellen looked straight at me. She did not glance at the man.

"You may return to your table now," the girl's voice said, and we followed her down the Pullman passage, the burrow, the curtained aisle to our table.

Ellen's sandwich and coffee, both sending up spirals of steam, like breath, were waiting. My drink seemed to be breathing, too, but with cold.

"Was it all right?" Ellen asked pleasantly.

"It wasn't anything."

"What was it like?"

I said, "It was like a booth at a county fair. It was like a mild electric shock—that's all." I wished I could speak to someone else who had stood inside the cabana. I would have asked—that moment I would have asked, "What did you choose?" I would have asked the question more loudly than Ellen ever shouted, identifying her passage among the passage of other human beings. But no one stood beside our table.

"I'm glad we didn't go in together. I hate things like that. All that stuff, honestly!"

"It is probably just as well," I said, drinking, knowing I would not ask anyone, "What did you choose?"

"I don't look as old as that waitress, do I? I don't really look that settled down and tramped under and long-time planted. Do I, Harold?"

"No," I said, making the word a long word.

Ellen said her sandwich was very good. She said the coffee was bitter. She said she had ordered a new storm door for the back porch. We said nothing more than we always said in restaurants or at home or at a party. We did not speak of the place we had found until after I had paid the check to a man in the hall and we were in the car once again. I did not look for the girl in a yellow skirt.

"We didn't have to go, did we?" Ellen said. "It wasn't even named *Noir*."

"Most of the cars are still in the parking lot," I said.

I pressed the starter button and guided the car along a painted arrow.

"Turn on the heater, Harold. I'm freezing."

"That time in high school—" I cleared my throat. "What did you say when you made the important announcement or speech or whatever it was?"

"I haven't the slightest idea. It was silly of me to remember it at all. All that stuff!"

The arrow was leading us out farther up the old Richmond Road, quite close to our own house, in fact.

"It was very interesting, the Cafe Noir," Ellen said. "You're not to mention it again, not so long as we both shall live. Promise me, Harold. Cross your heart."

I promised.

She gave no indication that she was planning to take the sleeping pills which would end time for herself, and, in a way, for me. I have not driven out the old Richmond Road any more, although I suppose the Cafe is still there. I do not say that Ellen's way was wrong.

If You Don't Go Out the Way You Came In

Walter Hoyton, Lexington, Kentucky, had been late for the first session of the Association of American and English Scholars meeting in New Orleans. He was late because he had stopped at the hotel bar and ordered three Manhattans, one right after the other. "It was an unscholarly thing to do," Professor Hoyton said to himself, even while he was drinking, already forgetting that he was disappointed not to find somebody he knew in the bar. "But I felt I needed strength to face my fellows," he said, as he burst the second cherry against his upper partial plate. And he said, "Keats," to himself. He could not recall the direct quote about bursting the grape, although he knew the words as well as he knew his own name: Dr. Walter Hoyton, Lexington's only representative to the A.A.E.S. He felt beautifully detached from Kentucky and the pettiness of an academic world.

"It was an unscholarly thing to do—*three* of them," he would say, and Ruth would smile efficiently at him over her needlepoint, and the people from upstairs, or the graduate students—whoever was in for the evening—would begin to laugh before the story was under way. Somebody—one of the girls—would say, "Nobody tells stories better than Dr. Hoyton," and somebody else, gently moving a bottle of beer to stretch himself full length on the serape by the hi-fi, would comment on the fact that fabulous experiences were always happening to Dr. Walter Hoyton.

But the lecture was far from a fabulous experience. Dr. T. A. F.

Hamilton was reading his usual paper on Melville when Walter arrived at the dingy auditorium. "So this is where I'm to spend the next two and a half days, I said to myself," Walter said to himself as he slipped into the next to last row. He had thought the row was empty. "Excuse me," he said to the man whose legs he bumped.

The man rose to let him pass. "Pardon *me*," the man said. His voice was very deep and quite Southern.

Walter smiled. He could never get over the feeling that a Southern accent was mere play acting. "Tell them about the convention, Walter," Ruth would say. Surely she would encourage him to talk about the convention. "Having been born in Vermont of God-fearing people with a very clipped speech . . . ." Walter thought. He wished Ruth had come with him.

The ride in the taxicab out to the university had been quite soothing—romantic, even, and soothing. "There I was riding through the soft tropical rain, and I thought of you people freezing at home. I thought about Ruth being excited over the first crocus." Ruth would have come with him if she hadn't been consumed with the League of Women Voters' campaign. It would have been nice if she had decided at the last minute to get on the train. He wished Ruth had said, "To hell with the goddamned League." Ruth cursed prettily. She was always shocking the young students; it was good for the kids to be shocked out of their Bible Belt complacency by people like the Hoytons. "Mrs. Hoyton, oh my goodness," one of the young girls would say, the color rising in her young Bible Belt face.

But Ruth had a sense of responsibility. It was impossible to imagine her hopping on a train in the middle of the night. The Hoytons were responsible people. (Ruth could say, "Tell them about that goddamned convention, Walter.") Even though Dr. T. A. F. Hamilton was being duller than his usual norm, one could sit in the dingy little auditorium in New Orleans and experience a sense of well-being, of completion almost. A convention delegate had a responsibility to his convention. It was a sad commentary on the state of academic responsibility that only the first dozen rows of the auditorium were filled. Walter shook his head. "A sad commentary."

He ran his hand down the back of his head. His hair was as thick as a rug. Almost every man in the first twelve rows was bald or balding. Some of them had even plastered long, long gray wisps over their center nakedness. They listened as intently as did the Southerner three seats away. They listened as if T. A. F. Hamilton had good sense. And after the lecture they would mount the steps to compliment the old man, hoping he would publish their little articles in his goddamned *Journal.* Those who had brought their wives would drag them up to the stage to say, "My husband admires your work so much."

Walter knew what the scattering of women would look like even before they turned their heads. Most faculty wives had outsized faces—"quadruple C or triple D," Ruth said. Ruth's face was a beautiful size. Ruth framed her beautiful face with expensive hats. Ruth wouldn't suck up to old Hamilton. Ruth said, "If he doesn't want to publish your Faulkner paper, to hell with him. What's publishing? You're a teacher, not an author. Who does that son of a bitch think he is?"

Walter Hoyton covered his mouth with his hand, glancing again at the Southerner. It was not fair of the Manhattans to lie heavily on his stomach, not when everything was so pleasant. But the Southerner would not have turned his head if somebody had belched through a megaphone. The Southerner was leaning forward in order not to miss one word of Hamilton's crap. He wore rimless glasses and a black suit and his hair was very thin in front. But the hair was cut short—you could say that for him. Walter wished the Southerner had brought his wife along. She would have a triple D face, and her hat would be bargain basement three years ago.

"The scholars may be scholars," Walter's voice would say to the guests who smiled within the charcoal and oyster walls of Lexington. "They may be scholars, but they're not gentlemen." He would run his hand over the carpet of his hair. "And there I was, a non-conventional man in the midst of a convention."

"Oh, Dr. Hoyton!"

"But even this would pass away, I thought, even this." Walter chuckled. He would chuckle when he told the story at home. "Even this."

And, blessedly, Dr. T. A. F. Hamilton's paper did pass away. The old man was at last massaging his manuscript and bobbing his round head awkwardly at the audience. He turned his great body from right to left, as if he stood in a shower stall, bathing in the applause.

The Southerner was making a great deal of noise with his large hands. Walter decided that the man taught in a small denominational college in some place like Alabama. Dr. Hoyton tapped his hands together three times, gently. He took his hat from the seat beside him, even though a rather brilliant question on the relationship of Faulkner and Melville sprang to his mind. Perhaps it was the soft spring night that waited outside, or his touch of indigestion, or the embarrassing intensity of the man beside him, but he was determined to leave. He would stand in the quiet rain and whistle for a cab; he would drop in at one of the publishers' parties for a couple of quick ones; and he would write a note to Ruth to let her know he had arrived safely.

"And now if there are any questions?" Dr. Hamilton still clutched his manuscript.

"I have found in my own study of Melville," Moore of U. T. began, licking carefully at each word. Sometimes it was difficult to love one's fellows.

Walter Hoyton uncrossed his legs.

He should have gone out the far end of the aisle, of course. "If you don't go out the way you came in, you'll have bad luck," his mother always said—thirty years ago she said it. Her bland face frowned as seriously over one superstition as another. "Everything was a religion with my mother," Walter thought as he crouched to slip out. It was not a very quotable quote, and he had no notion why he remembered his mother's foolish face. "Excuse me," he said to the Southerner.

"You're leaving?" the man whispered, rising slowly. He was tall. And his glasses . . . The glasses were not facsimiles of the glasses which Reverend Hoyton wore in Vermont, the better to see the terror on his congregation's face. But foolishly, goddamned foolishly, Walter remembered his father's glasses. "You're leaving before the questions and answers?" the man's voice was so resonant, even in a whisper, that the whole congregation could have heard him.

"If you'll excuse me," Walter said. It was quite laughable, and he wondered what he would do if the man refused to allow him to leave. For a moment of comic panic, Walter thought of breaking into a cough. On occasion he had left his father's church with a feigned coughing fit in order to walk around the white building and look intently at the blue Vermont sky.

"I'll go with you," the man was saying, and his breath was sweet, and he was following Walter into the lobby of the building, smiling down at him.

"You aren't a scholar," the man was saying. It was a question, of course. "You aren't a scholar?"

"As a matter of fact, I am. I am a delegate to the sessions. I attend several of these meetings every year." Walter ran his tongue over his lips. There was no reason under God's heaven to be explaining to the man. "I am a scholar, but I'm leaving."

"That fellow in there. He's really an authority?" It was another question. Walter was sure it was another question.

"He's an authority." Walter pushed gently past the man toward the great double doors which led to the street.

"And you like the school business?" The man spoke tentatively now.

"Very much." Dr. Walter Hoyton smiled and nodded. "Very, very much."

"That's what I wanted to know." The man was smiling, too.

Walter did not mean to be unkind. He started to ask, "Don't

you like teaching?" But Walter was not inquisitive, save in a scholarly sense. He loathed people who asked questions, personal or otherwise; it was part of his considerate nature. Ruth always said, "You're too considerate, Walter. You're too considerate for your own good."

So, Walter Hoyton waved his hand for the Southerner to precede him into the soft night. "It's a good life," he said quite naturally.

"There I was, looking in the face of this great Saint Bernard," Walter said to himself. He couldn't remember when he had considered his own height. Ruth Hoyton was four inches shorter than her husband. If she had wanted to leave the Saint Bernard, she would merely have said, "Move over, you ugly bastard," and walked away.

But the man, for all his bulk, was really rather shy. Teetering on the top step he spoke almost apologetically. "The reason why I asked you about that fellow . . . Well, I read *Moby Dick* last week. I don't mean to be critical, but it didn't seem like the man was much talking about the same book I read. If you know what I mean. I thought what he said was good, all right."

Walter laughed quite genuinely. He started to say, "I know what you mean." If he were positive the man was a teacher, he would have agreed. But he wasn't quite positive, and one didn't go around criticizing one's profession. He thought of saying, "Well, goodnight," and a cab would come along that very moment, splattering through the wet night.

The rain had stopped. The air was cool. Walter did not know why he had considered the night tropical. He hadn't met the Southerner, so it would be ridiculous to say, "It's nice to have met you."

"I'm Dr. Walter Hoyton, University of Kentucky." Walter extended his hand.

"I'm Edwin Tate." The man's clasp was powerful. He pumped one's hand almost as if . . . "as if the physical world could substitute for the intellectual," Walter thought, without quite knowing what his mind meant by the words. Of course he would not allow himself to rub his hand, "to rub back circulation," and then his mind said, "civilization," and he smiled broadly at Edwin Tate.

"I'd be pleased if you'd let me take you where you're going."

"As a matter of fact . . ." But no taxi was in sight, and he certainly did not want his fellows of the A.A.E.S. to find him awkwardly whistling in the deserted street, not when he'd left before the questions.

"I know you're busy," Edwin Tate said.

"As a matter of fact, I'd appreciate a lift." The word *lift* was not Walter's word. "There I was, taking words from another drawer of vocabulary. The man was powerful, I tell you, real powerful personality, as we say in New Orleans."

Walter matched his steps to the man's long stride. It was simple to keep in step, and, obviously, the man was embarrassed now over his presumption. Edwin Tate said it was cool, and Walter said it was very pleasant, and they were under a street light beside a black Chevrolet. "I've been looking forward to the speech tonight," Edwin Tate said, unlocking the door on Walter's side.

"I was just going to ask if you'd like to drop in on one of the publishers' parties. We can meet everybody, and the liquor's good." Walter felt sure the man was a teacher, but he wondered, suddenly, if they drank at small denominational colleges in Alabama. "They can be pretty dull, of course, but generally . . ." He did not stop smiling, even though it was difficult to imagine Edwin Tate in the smoky hotel suite beside the publisher's representative. The representative would be in his shirtsleeves; he would say, "I used to teach school myself," and he would urge Edwin to take off his coat. But Edwin Tate looked as if he had been born with his coat on. And his glasses—those goddamned, old fashioned glasses.

"That's very nice of you." The door was finally opened. Edwin Tate stood back, the light bright on those funny glasses.

"Maybe you aren't interested . . ." Walter began, but the man was already going around to the other side. The representative would tell the first joke, followed by the hierarchy—professors on down, increasingly specific of man's bodily function. A joke about making love on an ironing-board would sound very vulgar in the non-academic voice of Edwin Tate.

Mr. Tate closed his door gently.

"It's just a party, and there are a number of them." Walter was not apologizing. It was only that Edwin Tate made no effort to start the motor. "Like a bump on a log," Walter's mother would have said.

"Maybe the professors remember that night in New Orleans when they make out their bookstore requisitions—that's all, no commitment." Walter realized that he spoke as if he himself belonged to another profession and New Orleans were a thousand miles away.

"It's all right." Edwin Tate finally lowered his blinking eyes. Perhaps he even shrugged. And then he said, quite swiftly, "I'm a preacher. It's what I wanted to talk about. I'd appreciate a lot talking about it."

Automatically—it was completely automatic—Walter said, "I'm sorry."

Reverend Tate said, "I think I'm sorry, too."

They were laughing, actually laughing into each other's faces. "It was macabre, I tell you, the two of us laughing at each other. Not *at. With.* I'm sure *with* is the word."

"I'm thinking about giving up the ministry. That's why I came tonight. I read in the paper where you were having this meeting. I wanted to see what a bunch of teachers were like." Reverend Tate was not laughing any more. He had started the motor, the black car had already moved far away from the street light. "I figure a man ought to be in the place he fits best. You've only got so long. I've been preaching since I was seventeen—I never knew anything else."

"I have respect for the ministry," Walter said. You had to say something.

Walter said, "My father was a Methodist preacher—up in Vermont." He could not remember when he had mentioned his father, even to a friend. It was the glasses—those goddamned glasses. "I was reared in a preacher's household."

"Then you know what I mean." Walter Hoyton couldn't have pleased Edwin Tate more. The man was smiling all over himself, as if he'd found his twin egg. "You know exactly what I mean."

"It's a hard life," Walter said. "The pettiness." He was glad he had made the man happy; but he was uncomfortable. He was cold, too. It was the cold more than anything that bothered him. He held his teeth tightly together for fear they would chatter. The streets of New Orleans were as strange as the streets of a dream, and he remembered the bright nights of Vermont.

But they were on their way down town, all right, and there was nothing to worry about. In front of them the sky was very pink.

"This segregation business."

"It's good to hear a Southerner speak up."

"And this pettiness—like you say. Always the pettiness. The tea towels in the church kitchen, for instance." Reverend Tate drove very swiftly, but he drove well. "Martha and I have talked about it a lot. She's willing to go along with whatever I decide."

"Yes, yes," Walter said, clearing his throat. There was no need to answer the man; there was no need to listen to him. The black Chevrolet was a Protestant confessional booth. When the priest confessed to the laymen, every man was indeed an island. And across town the publisher's representative began the discussion of the relative merits of Scotch and Bourbon, and old Hamilton placed his manuscript in his briefcase, while Ruth said goodnight to the girls of her League.

"There's an elder in my church, for instance . . ."

Father Hoyton. Walter wanted to laugh in the dark booth.

"No, Walter," Ruth would say. "You're making this up."

"The things that happen to Dr. Hoyton!" The Bible Belt face would move closer to the sleek mahogany chair—they'd bought the chair in Mexico, eight hundred pesos, and there wasn't another like it in all the Bible Belt.

"Like I said, you've only got so long. Martha and I, we're almost thirty years old, both of us. The way I figure . . ."

Edwin Tate was lying. No one, absolutely no one, would believe that Walter Hoyton was a decade older than the man beside him. The ironing-board joke would have been no more shocking on the minister's lips.

When they were thirty . . . . They had already bought the brown china and the dining room furniture. He would like to tell Edwin Tate about the dining room. It was unfortunate that the confessor was uninterested in the state of his priest's bowels.

"You said it was a good life—that's what you said back there in the lobby. I wish you'd talk to Martha."

Reverend Tate had pulled the black Chevrolet to the curb. His face in the dashlights was as eager as a child's. His face was very young in the half light. "I know it's asking a lot, but I wish you'd talk to her. Just tell her what you told me."

"What did I tell you?" Walter's lips were dry again. "As dry as chips," his mother would have said.

"About the good life—you know. Meetings like this. You know."

"I'd be glad to," Walter said, for what else could a person say, and there was no room in the small booth for turning your mind around and around and around.

Reverend Tate turned the car in a U so swiftly that the tires wailed. "Like a banshee," Walter's mother would have said.

Reverend Tate said, "It's funny about people. I knew you were somebody I could get along with. People talk about coincidence. I don't mean to sound like a preacher, but I don't call it coincidence. I think it's providence."

"You are very kind," Walter said, which was a goddamned stupid thing to say.

"When you slipped in that row tonight, all humped over . . . . Look, I'm not much for formality. I want you to call me Ed. You don't know how sick a person gets of Brother and Reverend all the time."

"Of course . . . Ed."

"I've been calling you Walt to myself—all of the time we've

been talking. A member of my last church was named Walt—Chairman of the Board. Finest kind of fellow. You know, sometimes I think . . ."

Walter Hoyton wouldn't have minded talking to Martha Tate under any other circumstances. But one needed time to prepare a lecture. If there had been time, he would have worked out a really impressive *Apologia. Assertion. Assertion* was the word. He could make an essay of it, sophisticated but warm underneath, something for *The Atlantic* or *Harper's*. It would be infinitely more important to have a piece in *Harper's* than to appear every month in Hamilton's *Journal*, the son of a bitch.

But Ed Tate cheated, and there wasn't time to work out even an introduction. Perhaps they had been headed for the parsonage all the time. "Kidnapped," Walter Hoyton thought. The word "kidnapped" stood alone in his mind, undecorated by modifiers because the preacher didn't give you time to think.

"Walt, I can't tell you how much I appreciate this," the man said, opening the car door.

"Honey, this is Walt Hoyton. He's a professor at Kentucky University," Ed Tate said, closing the door of the parsonage behind them.

Martha Tate had a tea towel in her hand. She wiped it against the underside of her right arm, and she extended her hand. "I'm finishing up dishes, isn't that terrible? Ten o'clock at night and I'm just finishing up. Ed, I had a terrible time getting the children to quiet down. Frank was just awful. He kept teasing the big boys."

"How do you do," Walter Hoyton said to Martha Tate who was tall and blonde. And beautiful. She was beautiful in spite of her pale lips and her hair pulled back in a skinny knot. Her skin was ridiculously young. He was particularly conscious of her smooth skin stretched over her thin face. "I didn't know you had children," he said, like some stupid bastard in a bad play, feeding lines for the sake of exposition.

"Don't tell me I didn't mention the kids," the hero said.

"Ed's always talking about the boys. I keep telling him he talks too much about them," the heroine said. "He's always using them for illustrations in a sermon."

"Three boys. Three limbs of Satan." Ed Tate, smiling like a cartoon figure, placed his arm around his wife's shoulders. "Honey, we've been talking like sixty. There wasn't time to get it all said. Walt's father was a preacher. He knows all about preachers and teachers."

"My wife and I have no children," Walter said quickly.

"Oh," Martha Tate frowned. And then she said, "What are we standing here for?"

Ruth would laugh at Martha Tate's pitying "Oh." Ruth always said that mothers could not bear the thought of non-mothers. "If they didn't pity us, they'd go mad," Ruth told the graduate students. Walter Hoyton could hear his wife's laughter even in a New Orleans parsonage where "The Last Supper" hung over the mantel and the overstuffed furniture sagged beneath its flowered cretonne covers. "All the furniture suffered from double hernia," Ruth would say, and Ruth and the graduate students would laugh again.

Ed said they ought to have something to eat. Martha said she still hadn't got around to icing the cake—the icing was ready, but the children had been just terrible. And the kitchen was a mess. Ed said Walt knew what a preacher's house was like. "Walt knows about us," Ed said.

Ed Tate removed his jacket before he sat down at the oilcloth covered table in the center of the kitchen. "Sure you don't want to take yours off?" he asked as if he were a publisher's representative in a hotel suite.

"I'm very comfortable."

"It's right nippy out, isn't it?" Martha said.

Ed Tate told his wife about the evening while she moved softly over the worn linoleum—from refrigerator to sink to sideboard. They actually had a sideboard. Actually, a sideboard in the kitchen. "Walt says teaching is a good life."

Walter Hoyton cleared his throat.

"This is just a mix," Martha began to swirl chocolate icing over the white cake. She worked with a sharp butcher knife—no spatula for Martha Tate—but she worked professionally. "The *cake* is just a mix, I mean, I always keep a couple of boxes on hand, in case I get too rushed. But I don't think they're quite as good. The boys will eat anything, though."

"They take after their Daddy." Ed Tate smiled stupidly at his stupid wife. "I wish you could see those boys eat."

"See? See what I mean?" Martha asked.

Then there was talk of Fred and Fred's cough.

Walter Hoyton was angry. The anger rushed through his body like blood to a wound from a sharp knife. "Do you want your husband to leave the ministry?" The anger made his voice tremble.

"Whatever he thinks is right, I keep telling him. The boys will be in school next year, and I can work, part-time anyhow. Ed's determined to get a Ph.D. if he teaches. He wants to do it up right." The icing moved like lava, or like blood.

"But how do *you* feel about it?" Walter Hoyton was determined to make the stupid woman answer him. He spoke more loudly than he intended, but you had to speak loudly to a woman who turned to take cheap flowered plates from the dish drainer, who cut a fat cake with quick sharp strokes. It was important to force her into a statement. Ruth would certainly ask what the stupid woman *really* thought about the whole deal.

"Ed thought he was called to be a preacher but maybe he misunderstood the voice," she said, as if she were answering the question. "I think you can do just as much good in teaching as any place. More maybe, if you're not happy being a preacher. And Ed's right —we have a lot of intolerance in the church."

Ed Tate nodded at his wife's words, as if she were wise or clever.

"There are intolerances everywhere." Walter spoke carefully over his anger. He would say in the article for *Harper's* that naturally one found pettiness and intolerances everywhere, but he would make the words sparkle for *Harper's*. It was sufficient here, now, to line up the old arguments.

"We could go north, of course," Martha said to her piece of cake. "They even have Negroes in their churches up there."

"But the winters are cold," Ed said.

"That's true." She smiled at her husband.

"There are enough good things to make up for the pettiness. Time, for instance. You have time to enjoy life." He was almost shouting. "You have time." He was speaking the truth. Walter Hoyton had time to enjoy life, despite the committees, and the papers, and the goddamned freshmen. "There are lectures and concerts . . ."

"Ed doesn't like concerts."

"I don't have any music in me," Reverend Tate said as if he had received a compliment.

"I don't miss going. I play the piano enough for prayer meeting—that much. But we have a radio and television. She nodded toward the living room.

They are always nodding, the both of them, at each other, at the cake, at the guest they had dragged through the dark wet night. They nodded and smiled as they distracted themselves: Estelle had called about prayer meeting; the bulletin copy was due the next day; Martha had been trying to get Jackie all evening to ask about the Missionary program.

"The human spirit," Walter Hoyton said finally. Finally he said it, "The human spirit."

"That's right," Ed said, his mouth full of cake.

"A teacher is concerned with the human spirit!"

"Everything is, I guess, for people like us." Martha nodded and smiled as if to show Walt he was included with people like the Tates.

"A teacher is . . ." Dr. Walter Hoyton pressed his hands hard against the edge of the table. If he pressed a little harder he could turn the table over, the cake, and the flowered plates. They should have had something to drink—coffee, or water, or something. The overturned table would be more comic in a New Orleans parsonage if there had been liquid to mix with the bloody cake. It was ridiculous not to have had anything to drink.

"We could sit here the rest of our lives giving reasons—for anything," Walter said quietly. But he did not loosen his hold on the table. "If you don't go out the way you came in, you'll have bad luck."

They were listening now. The stupid goddamned people were listening and they didn't know what he meant. Martha Tate said, "I don't know what you mean."

"I guess I mean you don't want to be a teacher." Walter made his hands let go of the table. He moved his hands carefully, as if he tore off bandages.

"It's something we have to consider from all sides," Martha said.

"Your children. The degree—the degree is a long row." But it was foolish to bother speaking to the people beside him.

"Won't you have another piece of cake?" Martha asked. "I mean, *a* piece of cake. Ed's always getting after me for saying 'another piece.' I can't seem to remember."

"Thanks a lot, but no. It was very good."

"You aren't leaving?" Reverend Tate was stifling a yawn. Warmed and filled and empty of mind, the son of a bitch was ready for bed.

Walter stood up gracefully from the uncomfortable kitchen chair. He did not brace his hands on the table as did both the Tates.

"We certainly appreciate your little visit," Reverend Tate said, following Dr. Hoyton into the living room.

"We certainly do," his wife said.

"I'll take you back to your hotel."

"No need. I can get a cab or a bus." Walter smiled up at Reverend Tate. "Unless you'll accompany me to the drunken party?"

"I guess not tonight." Reverend Tate was chuckling. He did not seem offended at the thought of a drunken party.

"Lots of dirty jokes," Walter said, looking straight into the rimless glasses of the preacher.

"Honestly!" Martha Tate said. She was laughing and nodding at the door while her husband pointed to where the bus stopped.

"Honestly!" Martha Tate had said, just as they all would say when he told the story at home.

He certainly would tell the story. For a moment, there at the kitchen table, he had failed to realize what a really fabulous story it would make. For a moment he had thought, he had actually thought, that he would never tell the story to anyone, Ruth or anyone.

"And he let you take the bus back?" someone, moving still closer to the mahogany chair, would ask.

"He did."

"And you really talked a preacher into staying in the ministry?"

"I did. I did, before God."

"Honestly, Dr. Hoyton!"

And Ruth, the lines in her small face showing through the make-up, her hair splotched with dye under the severely modern floor lamp, would sound her goddamned tense laugh above the laughter of the others.

Mister Joseph Botts

At first Ernestine was completely overwhelmed with the wonder of the nieces and nephews. As she remembered it, she had been like a dancer, moving gracefully from one side of the stage to the other, turning her well-shaped head, as if in search, trying to decide on which of the children to kneel beside. But honestly, and it was very important to be honest now that everything had turned out as happily as a fairy story, honestly she had not known that Lucy would be the one.

Three years ago, at the Christmas family dining, one of Martha Nell's awkward little girls had twisted up her skinny face and asked, "Aunt Tina, why you be old maid?" Everyone around the table, even Lucy, had laughed as if the child were really clever.

Ernestine allowed the laughter to settle before she answered quite clearly, "I need to take care of my nieces and nephews—you're all my children." Some of the family had laughed again, but Lucy touched her arm and smiled. The candlelight caught the ugly class ring on the child's hand, the ring was wrapped with a bulge of adhesive: "Of course, Auntie," Lucy said. Ernestine touched the ring, twisting it a little so that the dirty adhesive showed more plainly. Lucy giggled and batted her eyes and whispered that the ring belonged to Mister Joseph Botts. "Not Mrs. Botts's son—at the bakery?" Ernestine asked, and Lucy nodded and twisted her shoulders. "Nice," Ernestine said, for it was all she could do to keep from crying.

She should have known then that Lucy was the one, but she had not known.

Ernestine Graham was willing to admit when she was wrong: Pappa always said it was a sign of wisdom. She had admitted, oh, time and again she had admitted to herself how wrong she had been about this person or that: the young men who used to call, for instance, with their weak mouths and common backgrounds; the nieces and nephews who wrote curt little notes at Easter and Memorial Day and Thanksgiving to explain their absence from the family gatherings. For a long time, just to show how mistaken a person could be, she had suspected that Martha Nell would be the other part of herself. It would have been real pleasure to possess Martha Nell, what with the child's mother glaring at everyone and insisting that she wanted to live in a house of her own. "You're welcome here. Pappa would want you here," Ernestine said. When they finally moved away, Martha Nell had leaned against her auntie and cried as if her little heart would break. Ernestine kissed the child until they were both out of breath. "Any time you're welcome," she called to the broad back of her sister-in-law; above Martha Nell's weeping her voice, kind and charming, rang so clear that even the neighbors heard.

She had known that morning, with a quiet infinite wisdom, that they would have to send Martha Nell's mother away. It had been a mistake, perhaps, for in no time at all Martha Nell was married to the little farmer up the road who smelled of the stable. Martha Nell was no better than the others: she fondled her awkward children and she missed a family dining whenever her little husband wanted to visit his folks in some godforsaken part of the state. It was all one could do to keep on being gracious and charming, for there was only Brother Albert's Lucy left, and Lucy had seemed the silliest of them all.

Six times Ernestine Graham had leaned over the cradle which her own Pappa had been rocked in. Six times she had wept helplessly at the birth of her brothers' children. Six times she had stood in front of the college chapel across the street, holding the new baby for its first picture, almost bursting with the joy of the moment. The pictures hung now around her mirror where she could see them every morning as she opened her eyes: Ernestine Graham dressed in ever changing styles for ever changing seasons, but ever young, stood at noon and smiled at the older waking Ernestine; the moments of the pictures crowded around her to bless the day, and she could hear Brother Albert and Brother Ed, their voices younger, speaking to her, "Smile," they said, and "Good, that's really good." After the picture-making she had led the way into the house for dinner, where Albert and Ed fought over who should seat her. They always had to wait the blessing for the sisters-in-law; the women would come red-faced and apologetic, pulling at their slip straps and smoothing back their dung-colored hair. After Pappa passed away, Ernestine herself, at the head of the table, smiled at the awkward women just as Pappa had smiled. "We wouldn't dream of going on without you," she always said, lifting a silver dish cover to make sure the food was not cold yet.

But even in the moments of triumph—when the boys quarrelled with their stupid wives, or when they came to borrow money, looking away from her eyes as if they were angry that Pappa had loved her best of all, even then, she had felt her throat contract with the hard breathing of the chase. Almost mystically she had known that some day she would grasp the other part of herself which, even in triumph, ran like a rabbit from the hound.

After the Christmas of the bandaged ring, after they'd sent Martha Nell's mother away and Ed had come back home to live, Ernestine Graham made arrangements to buy the Whalen place for Brother Albert. Ernestine Graham was fair; even the tradesmen said to her very face, "You're fair and square, and that's a fact." But she was tired. It was like—it was as if she raced to read ahead to see how the story ended—that was exactly what it was like. She had sent Albert and his tribe packing, trying to see the end of the story. She called to them, "You're welcome any time," but she was so relieved when she closed the door after them she could have lain down on the parquet floor. She did not even think about the ring on Lucy's finger.

For the first time in three generations the Graham house was quiet. Only Brother Ed, no trouble to anybody, poor thing, moved with her through the quietness—he was clumsy sometimes against the furniture or the stair rail, weak with the drink in him, his breath smelling up the place, but he was beautifully quiet and Ernestine was grateful, for she was very tired. Even the family dinners were a drain on her, but nobody bothered to sense it, of course. The candlelight shone on the faces around the table and the faces moved as if under water; she was cold and afraid because a person couldn't really see ahead to know how a story would turn out; somebody kept adding more pages to the book: Lucy kept adding more pages.

Ernestine tried not to look at the child's face. She tried to tell herself she had lost all of them and it didn't matter. But Lucy seemed to shout, "Catch me. Kneel beside me, Aunt Tina." Ernestine did not mean to allow her eyes to creep toward the girl, but the life in Lucy shimmered, like heat on the horizon; she moved her hands and her body, catching the light of attention; one could not look away for long.

Lucy said, "Yesterday at the Easter service, I had the most beautiful compliment. Alec said I looked like you." Lucy said, "I could die over missing the Memorial Day dinner. I hadn't realized. I could die." Lucy said, "Sweetheart, let me look at you, how stunning you are," and Joseph Botts was followed by somebody named Brian, then twins from Virginia, and worst of all, the Tom something who came for Thanksgiving dinner and admired himself in the pier glass mirror. The bandaged ring was replaced by a silver basketball, a fraternity pin, and then another ring, diamond this time.

Then no ring shone. Suddenly no ring shone.

It was Christmas again. As usual one of them said they all had a lot to be thankful for, and somebody spoke of war, and Albert said he was grateful to have all his folks in the good old U.S.A. He said it was a mighty sad time for people like Mrs. Botts. Albert's wife, her mouth full, turned to her daughter. "Joseph's picture's in the morning paper, Lucy. They brought his body home to bury—clear across the ocean." Albert's wife said, "Lucy was kind of sweet on him once."

Ernestine watched Lucy's face carefully. "Yes, I saw the picture," Lucy said. "He was an awfully nice boy." The maid passed the escalloped oysters; Ed tried to serve himself and Lucy lifted her young hands to steady the silver casserole. Lucy's hands were naked. Ernestine felt her own face move, as it had not moved since the little farmer took Martha Nell away, almost as if she were going to cry. "Mister Albert is ready for a beaten biscuit," she said to the maid, and her voice was breathless. Lucy lowered her eyes to the dish. "Coffee for Miss Martha Nell," Ernestine said, and she wanted to shout to all of them, "Quit dawdling. Can't you see what's going to happen?"

"It's not as if you were still going with Joe Botts, or anything, is it?" Martha Nell asked.

Lucy shook her head. Albert's wife said, "She's been looking peaked for a couple of days. I figure it's that Tom." Albert's wife laughed, and the food in her mouth was like dough.

"Do you remember the time when Pappa took us all to the State Fair?" Ernestine began. She could tell the story without thinking, and Albert would interrupt when she got to the part about the ferris wheel. She turned her well-shaped head from one side of the table to the other, and Lucy smiled.

After dinner was over (Lucy's stupid mother was enough to drive a person crazy; she kept picking at the candy pudding when everyone else was through), Ernestine led the way into the parlor. Beside her was Lucy. "I want to talk to you," Lucy whispered, and Ernestine pretended not to hear, for she could not speak above the joy in her throat. "I'll wait upstairs. I want to talk to you," Lucy said.

Ernestine knew the child would be in the blue room, but she opened the other bedroom doors first, stopping to look at the pictures around her own mirror—the picture with Lucy was the loveliest of them all, she should have known that Lucy was the one. The girl lay on the bed where she had slept when they all lived together. The other Lucy lay on the bed. Ernestine frowned: it was difficult to separate the child crying in the blue room from the child in the picture but Lucy was one person. "Lucy, Lucy, Lucy," Ernestine sang, and the child was in her arms. "Child, child," Ernestine whispered and after a while the crying stopped.

Ernestine moistened her lips with her tongue. She spoke softly, "I remember the first time you showed me his ring. It was a dining, just like today. The ring was too big and the candlelight . . ."

"No, Aunt Tina, not Joseph Botts." The girl moved her mouth against Ernestine's shoulder. Ernestine trembled, for she felt the words more than she heard them. "Tom, Aunt Tina, Tom. He asked me for his ring. I don't think I can stand it."

"Surely, sweet. Sweet, Lucy." Ernestine began to rock, back and forth, swaying the child and her words in the blue room which needed airing. "Yes, yes," she said, hardly hearing the little details of the story about Tom and a sorority sister, and the letter which somebody wrote somebody. "We're not given more than we can bear, honey," Ernestine said, and she thought of the dead soldier and his large hand which once wore a high school class ring. Perhaps, even then, she thought passionately of Mister Joseph Botts. "Yes, Lucy, baby, yes."

"And downstairs, all the family—it's so humiliating." Lucy cleared her throat in the quiet room. "They're bound to start asking questions."

Ernestine stopped rocking. She pressed her fingers against the child's soft shoulders. "Look at me."

The tears had washed Lucy's eyes bright. "I'm listening, Aunt Tina." She was no older than her first picture.

"We'll go down together, that's what we'll do. We'll work it out, Lucy, you and I. It's going to be all right. You're my girl, Lucy."

The child held up her face to be kissed. She said, "You're good, Aunt Tina. You're so good to all of us."

"No, Lucy, it's not goodness," Ernestine said, just as she had always said to Pappa. She closed her eyes. At the last, Pappa's smile was twisted by paralysis. "You're my flesh and blood," Ernestine said again, and she wished she would never have to turn the page of the moment.

Holding the child's hand Ernestine told them all: "Lucy's given Tom back his ring. She decided he wasn't good enough to marry a Graham."

"What's this?" Albert said, and Albert's wife, wallowing in Pappa's chair, began, "Now, Lucy, I've told you . . ."

"Lucy has been very brave," Ernestine said. "You're not to bother her with a lot of foolish questions. This is important."

"Well, honestly, I'm sure," Albert's wife said.

"We'll have more coffee now. Martha Nell, please pass the napkins." Ernestine felt the hard pressure of Lucy's young hand. She wished the hand wore a dead ring to bite into their flesh.

But there was no need of a token between them. Lucy herself said, "I'll see you tomorrow. I'll drop in tomorrow morning." It was always Lucy who made the arrangements for their meeting, right to the last. "I'll see you tomorrow," Lucy said. Nobody could say that Ernestine had pursued the child.

Tom and the sorority sister (Ernestine could never remember her name) were married on the day after college reopened. Snow covered the earth. "We'll go up to my room," Ernestine said when she saw Lucy's face. "Ed's not feeling so well this afternoon." The child did not answer, and Ernestine said, "We'll have tea in my room. It will be cozy against the snow."

Lucy sat in the flowered chintz chair by the west window. She said, "The cookies are good. Did you get them at Mrs. Botts's?" She said, "Thank you, no more." Then, suddenly, she said, "Talk to me, Aunt Tina. Please, talk."

Of course, sweet." Ernestine moved her rocker so that the child's head was framed by the window. "Let me see . . . Did I ever tell you about the time . . ." It was important to tell the stories well, of Pappa's being elected mayor, and Ed's 80-yard run against Louisville, and the celebration when Albert came home from his war.

Even if Lucy were not listening she would remember the stories with pride, as sleepers on winter nights remember the words whispered by lovers.

"Really, I've never heard that part," Lucy said as if she were listening. The sky behind her head was lemon and mauve and gray. The college chapel across the street slipped slowly from its squareness.

"Tom got married this morning." Lucy did not move her head. Ernestine was conscious of the presence of color behind the paper-thin chapel, but she could not name the color. "Aunt Tina, did anything like this happen to you?"

"Lucy, dear." Ernestine rose, gracefully without touching her hands to the arms of the chair, and moved around the room; she lowered the blinds, blotting out the memory of color in the south, and the presence of color behind tree branches and the college buildings. "There were always young men around the house," she said slowly; then, with a rush of words, "Pappa and Albert and Ed, they were always so careful."

To Martha Nell she would have said, "No, nothing like this ever happened to me." She would have told Martha Nell that she hadn't minded at all when the unworthy young men left the house and climbed into their fancy buggies, never to come back. A girl didn't have to be in love, just to *be* was enough, Ernestine always said, and the boys and Pappa had complimented her on her good sense. "The house was always exciting, full of company; and, then later, it was good to take care of Pappa." Ernestine's hands trembled as she turned the buttons of the vanity lamps, for Pappa had loved her best of all.

But Martha Nell had never said, "Please tell me, Aunt Tina, did somebody like Tom happen to you?" Martha Nell had never called for help. "Please." Lucy tramped the word in the snow, for Lucy needed to hear of pain. "Help me," Lucy called.

"I've never mentioned it to anyone before." Ernestine closed her eyes. "There was somebody. Don't ask me his name."

"Was it like Tom, Aunt Tina?"

Ernestine heard the child move as brightly as fire in the dark room.

She was in the dream; it was her turn to recite, but she could not remember a single word of the reading; backstage the elocution teacher had lost the book and the audience moved restlessly and one man rose to go. Ernestine Graham ran back and forth in her mind like a dancer; she could no more see the faces of the young men who wore stiff collars and flowing ties than she could outline the face of an idea, like love or even death. "He wore a stiff collar and a flowing tie," she said. She could see only Pappa's face, a young Pappa on the horse they had shown at the State Fair.

Ernestine described Pappa's face against her closed eyelids, for the child stood beside her and her young breath was warm. "He was tall and thin. His hair was black and soft and curled," she said, and she opened her eyes. Tears stood in Lucy's eyes. "His hands were especially beautiful."

"He was taken away, and I loved him." Ernestine spoke very softly, praying that Lucy would not hear the words if they were wrong.

This time she had remembered the recital piece and she had spoken beautifully, for there was the sound of applause and the man who had started to leave called, "Huzzah," and stood in tribute. Lucy pressed her face against Ernestine and called her name.

In the triumph Ernestine dared to say, "I loved him, Lucy—the way you loved Joseph Botts."

The color of the world outside pressed against the closed blinds. Ernestine Graham fingered the top button of her blouse. The man who called "Huzzah" wore the dotted newspaper face of Joseph Botts whose body had been flown across the ocean.

"Whatever do you mean?" Lucy drew back, but the kaleidoscope with its colored fragments of the dream did not move, and the plane mirrors still reflected the image of Joseph Botts.

"That day, downstairs, at the dining table, you said . . . you said, 'This ring belongs to Mister Joseph Botts.' Your eyes were very bright, and you were happier than I've ever seen you, Lucy, honestly you were."

"Aunt Tina. That was such a long time ago."

"Three years, only three years, Lucy. As sure as faith I knew Joseph Botts was the one. I knew it, Lucy." Ernestine placed her hands on the child's arm, for beneath Lucy's voice and behind her face lay laughter. Ernestine held tightly. It was very important to heap words and bury the laughter which tried to rise even in her own throat. "I said to you that day, 'Nice,' I said, and it was all I could do to keep from crying, because I knew he was the one. But he was taken away, Lucy. And your Tom knew. Tom knew you never really loved him, not the way you did Joseph."

"Aunt Ernestine, you're hurting me; you're hurting my arm."

"You can get over losing a boy to somebody else—that isn't losing. But you can't get over really losing a boy, to death—I mean, the way we've lost. You don't lose a person when he goes on living. But when he's dead . . ." Ernestine let loose of the child's arm, as if she threw down a book or a shovel or even her own body after a race. She breathed heavily, but she was able to say, "You've been crying, for a month you've been crying for Joseph Botts."

The child's eyes were wide, her mouth was open. Her small fingers lifted to her mouth, as if to feel Ernestine's words on her own lips.

"I'm mixed up," Lucy said. "I'm all mixed up. I don't know anything."

"Baby sweet, you're trembling. You're my girl. We'll have fresh tea. We'll talk about Joseph together. We're together. We have each other, don't we, Lucy?"

The child lifted her wet face to Ernestine and the child almost smiled. Outside the bedroom door Ed stumbled in the hall, but the house was quiet.

Ernestine kneeled beside the child's chair. "Sweet, sweet."

"Joe . . . that's what I really called him." Lucy spoke as if she too moved in the dream. "And we really did have a lot of fun together, Joe and I. I hadn't remembered. We had so much fun."

"Tell me. Tell me, Lucy."

Lucy lifted her head quickly. Her eyes were afraid. "Wouldn't it be awful if he was the one?"

"We're not given more than we can bear, honey."

"I'm scared, Aunt Tina."

Ernestine's body ached with kneeling, but she did not move to touch the child.

"I didn't even bother to go to his funeral services. And all this time . . ."

"We'll make it up, some way, honey. We'll take flowers; that's what we'll do." Lucy began to move her head from side to side, as if she searched for a hiding place, and Ernestine had to sharpen her voice to pierce the girl's consciousness. "What flowers did he like? What flowers did he like best, Lucy?"

"He always made jokes, and he laughed a lot."

"My young man liked roses," Ernestine recalled. "Red roses, he liked, Lucy. Did Joseph Botts like red roses?"

"I'm trying to remember. Can't you see I'm trying to remember?"

"The picture in the paper—he looked like the kind of a boy who would admire roses."

"Maybe he did, maybe. I'm almost sure."

"Red roses?"

"I'm almost sure." Lucy pressed her hands against her temples. She seemed to be looking past the room. "There was a song." Lucy began to hum, but her song held no more melody than the car which passed on the street beyond the blinds. "He couldn't sing very well, but I'm sure it was about roses. I think it was." She hummed again, and no car passed. "I can't remember."

"We'll take roses, Lucy; that's what we'll do."

"He was crazy about Marilyn Monroe. I know that for sure. We went to see one of her old pictures two different times." The words dropped from Lucy's mouth slowly, as if they were pebbles dropped into the water of a dream. "And he liked red. He liked a red dress of mine."

"My young man favored red, too. It's almost funny, isn't it?"

"The second time we went to that show, he called real late. I slipped out and I wore the dress. I guess it was awful to slip out that way."

"It wasn't awful at all." Ernestine laughed as she thrust the pebbles quickly into the pocket of her mind before they ever touched the water. "Pappa and the boys would have skinned me alive, but it wasn't awful at all."

"And he liked to dance."

"Really, Lucy. It's too much of a coincidence, really. I know he was graceful, too, wasn't he?"

But Lucy did not go on to remember dancing. Suddenly, the child's face crumpled like a sponge, and Ernestine rose, as if from prayer, to call comfort into the room with, "There, there," and "Lucy, Lucy," knowing she had found the other part of herself. "Things work out, child. All things work together for good."

It was no time before the child was saying, "Do you know what I'm thinking about?"

"Yes, yes." Ernestine looked steadily at the girl's face, allowing her eyes to rest on the lines which would deepen, the mole, the faint moustache. She wished Lucy would say, "We're the same age, aren't we, Aunt Tina? Exactly the same age!" She had thought for a moment that the child was going to take the words out of her mind.

Lucy said, "Joe must be somewhere watching us."

"Of course he is, of course." Ernestine turned the child in a half circle toward the bed. She did not want the child to be frightened. Joseph Botts stood beside the vanity dresser which would hold the first jonquils, pale and handsome as winter sunlight.

"I feel better. I always feel better with you," Lucy said. "We must get out more, you and I. We'll go to the movies together, and tomorrow and the next day and the next—we'll do all sorts of pleasant things."

"We will hurry before the magic breaks," Ernestine said to herself. She was sure she had spoken to herself, for the child did not turn to the vanity dresser. Despite her charm, Lucy was the silliest of them all.

Perhaps, if they had gone straight to Mrs. Botts's rooms over the bakery, Lucy would have waited a little longer to lose the good part of herself. But Ernestine had not really expected her to last longer than spring, and a few days, one way or the other, didn't really matter. It was Pappa's phrase: "A few days, one way or the other." At the last he had said it, and he tried to smile, right at the very last, ever so grateful to her for easing his misery.

She had sensed the end in the beginning, but with Lucy she did not hurry the end. A quiet pleasure promenaded through the waiting. Mister Joseph Botts grew in favor and in stature. He smiled in the church and the post office and the book store and the college auditorium. Ernestine Graham, lying on her bed, smiled at the first jonquils on the vanity dresser. The whole world was decorated with the youth and love of Joseph Botts.

Ernestine had told Lucy so, the last day. "The whole town seems to have been redecorated—seeing it as you and Joseph saw it, I mean." Lucy had reached across the carved wood of the Sweet Shoppe table and touched her hand. It was a Judas kiss, of course, for in the very next breath she told of Nat somebody and his invitation to a dance. "I'm going. I'm going with him, Aunt Ernestine. It's all right, isn't it?"

Ernestine looked down at the table with its crude hearts and arrows and waving initials. She was quite sure she could find her own initials if she cared to look. She was not angry. She had planned with the utmost care not to be angry.

She said, she said only, "I've been promising Mrs. Botts we would call on her. If you are willing, of course."

But it was too late for the visit to do any good. Lucy looked angry, her eyes big and stupid, as if she would be glad to shoot a bullet into the heart of Joseph Botts. Lucy would have murdered Pappa, even if he hadn't been sick. Lucy would have enjoyed handing him the extra tablets to make him sleep into eternity. Lucy's confused anger was almost amusing.

Mrs. Botts, gray with flour, hovered over Lucy, handing her letters and snapshots and asking if she were quite comfortable, but it was all too late. At least the child had the decency to contain herself until they were back in Ernestine's room. One should be thankful for the child's veneer of refinement, one should not even bother to remember the child's loud voice, or her flaming cheeks. "That was awful. It was just awful to go there," she shouted as soon as they were home. "I don't ever want to go again, not ever."

"Mrs. Botts is Joseph's mother." Ernestine's voice was beautifully calm.

"I don't care. You can't keep on going around with dead people. You just can't."

"You've been talking to your mother, haven't you, Lucy? I thought you decided Joseph was to be our secret."

The child looked positively absurd, backing her way out of the bedroom, feeling her way against the wall, like a criminal, almost a murderer, slowly moving to the stairway, ready to turn and run as soon as her thin little hands reached the stair rail. "My mother said taking the roses was all right, she guessed, but . . ."

"What else did your mother say?"

"I don't remember. Honestly, I don't. Aunt Tina! It's not I don't appreciate all you've done for me."

"Today is the day for the roses, Lucy. Today is the day."

"You're mad at me, aren't you? About going to the dance with Nat. That's it, isn't it? But don't be mad. I just don't want to go to the cemetery any more."

"I've never told a soul about the roses. I've kept our secret, Lucy."

"You can have Joseph all by yourself."

Actually, the child said, "You can have Joseph all by yourself." Before she turned and raced down the stairway, she said the words, as if Joseph were hers to give. The stair rail, running under Ernestine's fingers was as smooth as silk, lifting her up, almost as if she flew to the door to call after Lucy. "Come back soon. You're welcome. Any time," she called with genuine cordiality. One could only pity the child. It was almost embarrassing to look at her thin little figure, knowing one had taken Lucy away from Lucy: the child's glittering youth had come off like a cloak in one's hands. It was sad for the child to be left with only the silly part of herself.

Ernestine brushed past Ed in the upstairs hall, and closed the door of her room. She unfastened her blouse quickly, tearing the top button in her haste. She did not bother to lift her eyes to make sure Mister Joseph Botts, no longer wearing either his stiff collar or his flowing tie, waited for her.

The Third Ocean

Bill was three and Tim was a baby when the Travises began going to the ocean every summer. They had not missed one summer in twelve years, and now their ages were multiples of three: four and five times three, and thirteen and fourteen times three. William Travis did not mean to make anything of the fact. He thought of their ages while he was driving slowly behind three long trucks outside Grafton, West Virginia. He thought of saying, "We are multiples of three," but he did not want Emily to say, "What a silly thing to think of," and so he said nothing. Instead he passed, without caution, one of the long trucks, and Emily said, "William, please."

But Tim mentioned their ages the first afternoon at Delmont Beach. The four of them were building a sand castle. Tim said, "You know what? We're all three times something." He spoke as if he were speaking to the turret. He said, "And three is very mystic. Red, white, and blue; past, present, and future; and Father, Son, and Holy Ghost."

Emily said, "Really, Tim!"

Bill said, "How cloddy can you get?" but he spoke without heat. "And chocolate, vanilla, and strawberry." He scooped another handful of sand from the base of his castle wall.

William said, "I think that's very interesting, Tim." He was pleased with his son's observation, but he was determined to find no significance in the chance of their similar thoughts. "The air is soft," William thought. But if the boys and even Emily should have said in chorus, "The air is soft," he would have found no significance in the chance of their repetitions. "It is a lovely afternoon," William thought.

Bill's wall collapsed. "Good gosh. I'm too old to be playing in the sand. For gosh sakes."

Tim said, "Because of the threes, this is a *very* important summer."

"Every summer is important." William spoke casually. Already the sand and sun and water had made him feel casual.

Tim said, "But this is *especially* important because of the *threes*."

Bill said, "I think maybe he's really flipped." He stood up and adjusted the snap-on glasses he wore over his regular glasses.

"Here now," William said casually. The shafts of Bill's glasses were pale against his brown skin, but the snap-on lenses were circled in black. From William's angle the boy looked like a vast insect, or a man from space. "Here, here."

Bill brushed the sand from his trunks onto Tim. Tim hit at Bill's legs. Bill kicked at Tim's part of the castle, but the turret did not fall. Tim said, "Look at what you almost did, crazy." Bill said, "D'ja hear what he called me?" Tim said, "That's good enough for you."

William allowed his eyes to study Emily's profile. She was always beautiful. And she knew how to handle the boys, certainly. And she had not reacted at all to the word *crazy*. Last year she would have jerked her head toward him, suddenly, three lines between her eyes.

He was quite well now. He had worked too hard, enlarging the store and its sales force, arranging new accounts, reorganizing the books. The chaste signs on the windows were true, finally. The signs finally said, *William Travis*. For years after his father's death he had kept the name *T. R. Travis and Son* on the stationery, and the windows, and the accounts. But if ghosts walked, T. R. Travis would not recognize the store now. William had a right to be proud of his work. He had only worked too hard.

It was fatigue. A year ago last February the doctors in Cleveland had agreed it was only fatigue. In three weeks William Travis had learned to look more easily at the world. In three months he had almost learned to reaccept himself, and the world of Madison, Kentucky, and the world itself.

A person could not blame Emily's fear of her husband's sickness any more than a person could blame himself for fatigue. Emily lived in a single world of *twos*: good and bad, Catholic and non-Catholic, sane and crazy. Fatigue swam dark in a sea of threes, once, over a year ago. But now the boys could call each other *crazy* quite naturally. Even Emily was not bothered by the word. William was not bothered by the word, or the boys, or multiples of three, or even the thought of a great shark who swam somewhere, always. Emily was a good companion. A man of forty-two could not expect to be a lover forever. Surely many wives refused themselves to their husbands, even young wives, even their young husbands. And sharks swam in every season.

The old man at the Shell Service Station, back in Madison, was the first person to mention the summer sharks. When William was signing the credit slip for the gasoline, the grease job, and the new tire, the man said, "They're certainly having a lot of trouble with those sharks."

William had not dreamed of the great shark in months. Perhaps he lifted his head suddenly to the old man, but he was not troubled by the man in gray overalls who spoke of sharks. William watched his own hand steadily make his own name. He finished making his name before he asked the man where they were having trouble.

The man raised his hand to his ear. William had forgot, for a moment, that the man was deaf. William spoke loudly, "I said, 'I haven't seen a newspaper!' "

The man pushed at the bill of his cap. "I forget just where it was. Somewhere along the East Coast."

William had meant to tell the man that they were going to the ocean. He liked to say, "We are going to the ocean." Landlocked in Kentucky he had never said *beach*, or *shore*, or even *the coast.* Old Miss Markham, who had worked in Children's Wear ever since

William wore children's wear, teased him about saying *the ocean.* "I don't know why I say it, Miss Markham." She was the only employee left from his father's time. He could not keep from feeling awkward in her presence. If one of his own clerks had teased him about saying *the ocean,* he would have said that naming *the ocean* made him grow taller. He had an easy relationship with the men and women he had hired himself.

The service station man's name had slipped his mind. "We're going on a little trip," he said. He liked the quiet slow man. Sometimes in their brief conversations William swore a little, and the quiet man always said, "You're goddamned right, Mr. Travis," and they smiled at each other.

"Have a good trip, Mr. Travis." The man knew everybody's name, just as T. R. Travis had known everybody's name a long time ago. "And be careful."

"We're just going for a week. This year I can't get off any longer." He did not say, "We are going to Delaware." He did not say, "I am afraid to try the ocean for longer than a week."

They had spent one night on the road as usual. They arrived early Wednesday afternoon as usual. Everything was almost as usual, but they knew where they were going to stay. When they were younger they had merely ridden to the ocean and found a cabin. Now they preferred the comfort of a reservation. One of Emily's Vassar friends had given them the name of Delmont Beach and Mr. Meigg. Emily kept close touch with her past. Or perhaps her past was always present. William regretted that Emily had never met his father.

He did not miss a turn in arriving at Ocean Side Cottages. The cottages did not view the ocean, but they were on the ocean side of the highway: twelve little box cabins facing each other and a square gravel driveway. They did not look unlike the postcard Emily's friend had sent, and the rent was remarkably inexpensive. Emily delighted in economizing on vacations. "We can have luxury at home. And you meet more interesting people off the beaten path," she was always saying. "This is very adequate," Emily said. And there was Mr. Thomas Meigg, the proprietor of Ocean Side Cottages, sweeping the front step of one of the cabins as they drove into the square.

"I bet that's ours," Tim said.

"Bet you anything," Bill said.

It was number three, and only incidentally, their cabin. Tim said, "See?" and Bill said, "See what, silly? I'll beat you in the ocean."

Mr. Meigg leaned his broom against the clapboard wall. "Welcome to Ocean Side." His voice was a harsh whisper, and his face was so scarred that it was difficult to look at him straight. "You made good time."

Tim shook Mr. Meigg's hand, and said, "It's very nice to meet you." Bill shook his hand, and then looked away, humming under his breath. William found himself ridiculously moved by the boy's sudden manners. Bill even stood back to let Tim go first into the orange shellacked walls. Emily, of course, was entirely gracious.

"Fine. Yes, this is very attractive. Yes," she said in the sparsely furnished partitioned box which was cabin number three. "Twin beds," she said, as if she had not specified twin beds in her letter to Mr. Meigg. "And a stove, and sink. We can have our breakfasts here. How nice."

William tried to imagine the partitions to the ceiling, making two bedrooms, a family room, and a bathroom. Parents who were lovers would need to love cautiously within these walls. And men who cried out their nightmares could not cry privately. But he was being foolish. He had promised Emily he would not bother her any more. And he had not dreamed of the shark in over a year, not since Florida.

"You'll want to sign the registry," Mr. Meigg said. "And towels. I'll give you more towels if you come on up to my place."

Mr. Meigg's cottage was closer than the cabins to the ocean, but still hidden from the ocean by the dunes. Mr. Meigg whispered that the news didn't look very good but the weather had been fine. He said he liked August at the beach better than any other month. He said he had a place in Florida, too; incidentally, Mr. Meigg would be glad to have their business if they happened to find themselves in Florida.

"You in the war?" Mr. Meigg asked as he handed William the plastic book entitled *Friends Who Called.*

"A little while," William said, looking straight at Mr. Meigg. "I had a short trip."

The man lifted his hand to his scarred cheek. "Then we don't need to talk about it any."

"Of course not," William said, knowing he would not speak of Mr. Meigg's war to Emily; he did not want her to consider Mr. Meigg an interesting person off the beaten path. "I'm sorry," William said, wishing for other words.

"That's fine," Mr. Meigg said.

"We were in Florida last year." William began to write his name. At New Smyrna. In June. But only for a couple of days. We ran into a lot of jellyfish."

The Portuguese Men of War were deformed pink and purple balloons, covering the beach at New Smyrna the morning after the Travises arrived. For two days the Travises sat in a cove and sunned. "Please, please let us go in the ocean," the boys said.

"Get hold of yourself," Emily said. "You're well now. The doctors said you were well."

"They're just jellyfish," the motel proprietor said.

They had made love the first night in the motel. It was the last night they had made love.

"Please let us go in, just once."

"Your father is making the decisions," Emily said, but it was Emily who made the decisions after Florida. "We're too old for all that stuff any more, William. I think it upsets you. We're too old to be like silly young lovers, William."

"Please, please," the boys said.

But William had insisted that they go back to Madison, Kentucky. He could not say why; he could not remember why. There had been no rumor of sharks in Florida.

"They blow away," Mr. Meigg said.

"Florida has some fine beaches."

Mr. Meigg lifted his hand to his scarred ear. William raised his voice. He would raise his voice all week to Mr. Meigg even if the man were not hard of hearing.

"Hurry, hurry," the boys called outside the picture window of Mr. Meigg's house that faced the sand road.

"Hurry," Emily said. She looked very young. She wore her white suit. Emily owned many bathing suits.

"I'm hurrying," he called, as he closed Mr. Meigg's register. "But don't wait for me."

First he hung the four yellow towels carefully on the bathroom racks. T. R. Travis always said that his son got his tidiness from his mother. But William could barely remember his mother. She was a gray squirrel coat and the odor of violets. William and his father lived in the big house on Court Street for all of their lives together. A series of housekeepers walked through the parlors and the kitchen of the big house. And always there was Miss Markham of Children's Wear, advising and consoling and occasionally coming for dinner in the oak paneled dining room. William did not really believe that Miss Markham had been his father's mistress. Small towns always insinuated relationships; he had managed to separate himself from the insinuations of Madison a long time ago.

He took the four suitcases out of the station wagon. He picked up the clothes Emily and the boys had left in the bedrooms. Emily's clothes made hieroglyphs perhaps: she did not have the memory of a gray squirrel violet mother. William started to pull down the cracked green blind: the blind was crossed and curved and dotted, almost as if it were deliberately patterned. A light behind the blind would pattern the ceiling with constellations: "There's Venus," "And there's the Milky Way," "And even Mars," lovers could tell each other. But Emily had obviously undressed without pulling down the blind. They were at the ocean. A man discovered his body at the ocean; he became an anonymous body at the ocean.

William placed his folded sport shirt on the dresser. He hung his trousers on the rod which hung in the corner of the bedroom. He stepped into his athletic supporter and trunks. He turned back the beds for the night. The sheets were quite clean, almost blindingly clean. Ocean Side was all right. After the boys had said *Cloddy* and *Stinkoo*, or whatever words they were currently riding, they would say, "This is O.K. This is really O.K.," and Emily would speak naturally of *our house* and write a long letter to her Vassar friend in St. Louis.

He closed the screen door as carefully as if someone slept in cabin three.

He walked down the sand road, past Mr. Meigg's house, past three more cottages with screened porches and television aerials, the ocean pounding in his ears.

Twelve years ago he had first taken his family to the ocean—a South Carolina ocean. He did not feel any older than twelve years ago. He wore the same body. The body he wore had never really seen the ocean without Tim and Bill and Emily. He did not count the other ocean he had traveled as a young man in a troopship, to be wounded a little, to be hurriedly returned to Madison, Kentucky. He did not count the other ocean he had sailed as a child with his parents, searching through a winter for his mother's health. He had not really seen the ocean during the war or that other time, not the way he was going to see it now, not the way he always saw it with his family, except for the last time in Florida.

The third ocean was the only ocean.

He did not break his step as he mounted the rise of the dunes.

And there it was, exactly as he remembered it, the way it always was, lovelier than he remembered it.

Emily and the boys jumped in the breakers. They hung a moment against the sky.

"Hurry Daddy," Tim shouted.

William ran as fast as he could run toward the vast water.

He needed the ocean. He did not doubt his need, or his desire. He did not try to differentiate between the dark requirements of need and desire. The ocean was neither Emily, whom he remembered well, nor his mother he could barely remember. This ocean was the ocean.

He was fifty feet tall. The waves knocked him down because he allowed them to. He was stronger than any tide. He could swim to Portugal, if he cared to; he did not care to swim to Portugal. He lingered among the breakers because he wished to. He was knocked down because he wished to be knocked down. He neither doubted nor questioned his need or his desire. Tim had spoken of the *threes* because Tim happened to think of the threes. Everything that happened was a coincidence, or nothing was a coincidence, and neither way mattered presently or finally. *The third ocean is.* Values lay in living—that is what the doctor in Cleveland said, that was the way to look casually at the world. If William Travis thought of the natures of number or mystery, he thought of them casually.

For four days the ocean did not disappoint him, not with a third, or a ninth, or a thousandth wave. He read without much concern of sharks in waters that bordered New York or Maryland or Georgia. He deliberately bought newspapers at the doors of restaurants up the highway. He did not avoid discussing the sharks with the elegant grandmother and her son and daughter-in-law who sprawled under the next umbrella, or the old couple who walked the beach three times a day, or the young parents who crowded the water, or Mr. Meigg who never came to the beach. "Haven't seen a shark since I been here, three years now," Mr. Meigg whispered, smiling. "They aren't going to scare me with their shark talk," the grandmother said, glaring at her very pregnant daughter-in-law, moving into the water to swim her graceful side stroke, returning gracefully: "Do you see any shark marks, Jennifer?" The old couple, holding hands, went into the water up to their thin knees. "Keep a sharp eye out. Sharp eye," the old lady said. The two boys, whom Bill named County Snakes, fished every afternoon and evening for the sharks. "We'll get 'em," they told each other, hitching at their tight trunks. "We'll get us some."

Until Sunday the Travises left the beach only to eat. Every

morning William rented a chair and an umbrella from the two blonde young men who wore *Life Guard* on their tee shirts and drove a scarlet Jeep up and down the sand. "I can't feel they're much protection, those life guards," Emily said. "But they count change well." "Silly William," Emily said. "They'll life guard if they need to," he told her.

All day the Travises sat on the beach, rubbing oil on themselves, dipping in and out of the ocean. The boys were companionable; they did not quarrel much; "Come on in," they called, and William came. Emily joined them in fashioning a sand castle at least once a day. But most of the day she sat in the chair under the umbrella and wrote letters, and read, and did her nails. Most of the day William lay near her, out of the shadow of her umbrella, looking at the clean wide scenery.

"My, you're getting brown," she said.

"This is good for us, isn't it?" she said.

"The boys are sturdy, aren't they?" she said, waving her nails to dry in the salt air.

Once, on Saturday afternoon, she lowered her book and smiled gently at William. He did not mean to make anything of a wife's smiling at her husband. He wished she would reach out and touch his shoulder, but he did not wish deeply. And he had promised to leave her alone, before God he had promised. "We're not going to get a divorce, William. We will work out our human salvation," she said in the Florida motel. She had obviously prepared the words she was saying; perhaps she had even rehearsed the words before Father Baldwin back in Madison. "Look at me, William. We are husband and wife because we are married in the eyes of God, and because we are the parents of two children." "But the other night . . ." he said. "That was a mistake. We're going back to Madison, and we're not going to have any more of that . . . stuff. Look at me, William, and promise."

"You promised, you promised," she said the few times he had tried to forget or ignore his promise. "Before God you promised."

He had not challenged her God or his own promise. For a year now, because he was weak and dominated, or because he was strong and wise, or because, because, because: because a man had to work out his human salvation, he accepted Emily's edict and his own promise.

"We aren't a typical family any more," Emily said, smiling at Delmont Beach. "We're older than the other families now, aren't we? We're the oldest family all together at the beach."

"Oh I don't think so," William said, although he had noticed the young families that first afternoon even before Tim spoke of the *threes*. "The boys are fine."

Emily said, "At the ocean everybody used to be in their thirties and have two children. At the ocean we used to be everybody's age."

"Now they have four and they're still in their thirties." William's laughter sounded quite natural in the bright sun. "We like family beaches. We've always said so." He pushed himself up to sit in Emily's shade.

"Next year, Bill will probably be—I don't know, somewhere on his own." She was not smiling now.

"There's no reason . . ." William's eyes held Emily's eyes; he had to force his eyes to keep looking. "We've always said we liked our ocean because it wasn't Miami, or Virginia Beach, or . . . or Rehobeth."

"Of course we do. It's silly to think about." Emily shrugged. Her breasts moved in her white suit.

"In Florida . . ." William said, taking his eyes from Emily's breasts.

"You promised, William." Her voice was not unkind. "We promised each other we wouldn't talk about that any more. We've stopped talking about that time. That was part of your promise, William. You promised."

"Sure," he said.

Before she lifted the book from her lap, she said, "I complimented Mr. Meigg on Delmont. He said it was a fine place if you weren't wanting to *go* all the time." Emily laughed. "That's exactly what the man at Pauley's Island said."

"I know," William said, but his wife was reading.

"It's a lovely afternoon," the old woman said, and the old man nodded as if he had thought of the comment himself.

"Fine, fine," William said, stretching again on the sand.

In the evenings after dinner they walked, as they had always walked at the ocean after dinner. The boys ran ahead of them, sometimes lost, sometimes appearing suddenly behind them or at their sides, stamping stiff legged into the waves and out. Always they walked toward the flush of light at the edge of the sky, and always the boys suggested that they walk clear to the town ahead, Myrtle, or Santa Monica, or Rehobeth.

As usual Emily said they would save town for a rainy day. "There are always rainy days at the ocean," she said.

Sunday morning she took the boys to the early service at the little Catholic church up the highway. William lay on the beach by himself under a sky that held clouds a while, and the sun, and clouds, and the sun, and clouds. "Careful, baby, don't let the fish get you," the young mother with the lemon colored hair called to her toy doll-child. The clouds did not look like maps or elephants or human beings. "If I am not contented, I am thinking about the word contentment." *Catch, catch. Good morning. Lovely morning.*

"Mother says why don't we go to Rehobeth for lunch," Bill said.

"Maybe this is the rainy day at the ocean," Tim said under the sun.

He had slept. He had never slept on a beach in all of his life. The boys stood above him in their Sunday suits.

"I was asleep. I went to sleep," William told his sons.

"My how nice we look," the elegant grandmother said.

"Do you want to go to Rehobeth for lunch?" Bill asked.

"Fine, fine," William said. "Everything's fine at the ocean."

"Everything's fine at Rehobeth, but I'm ready to go home," Tim said.

"Home?"

"I mean our house. Our cabin, I mean." Tim laughed sputtering his popcorn. Bill laughed too.

They had eaten well; they had walked the boardwalk; they had placed dimes in machines to receive fortunes, and scarlet candy, and glass rings; they had ridden on the Sea Basket which tilted and twirled them against the sky; they had wandered in shops and bought pennants and cotton candy and souvenir flashlights. In Greshwin's Sea Knacks, Bill put his arm on Tim's shoulder as they studied an aquarium that contained sea horses. The proprietor smiled at the boys and went over to talk to them.

In the car Tim said, "That man said the father sea horse has the babies."

"He takes care of the eggs," Bill said. "He doesn't lay them."

"One father had five thousand babies last week and they all died."

"More like five hundred, or more like fifty," Bill said.

"But they all died."

"Why don't you turn on the radio?" Emily asked.

William turned the left knob, and after a moment he twisted the other knob until a newscaster's voice entered the car. His voice was young and apologetic. He spoke of another miracle in space.

"Hey, leave that," Bill said.

"Golly," Tim said.

The announcer had finished telling of the miracle. He told of the shells in Greshwin's Sea Knacks.

"That's where *we* were," Tim shouted. "What do you think about that? That's where *we were*."

"Everybody knows that," Bill said.

"And now for news of our area," the announcer said.

"Space is our area," Tim said.

"Hush up," Bill said.

It was not the coincidence of turning a dial three times that brought the shark into the car. They would have heard of the shark from Mr. Meigg anyhow. It was better to have heard of the shark first from the apologetic announcer.

At Indian Beach a shark had chased Mr. T. M. Robbins into the shore. Mr. Robbins escaped without injury. Mr. Robbins was swimming from fifty to sixty feet offshore. The shark was estimated to be at least nine feet in length.

"Where's Indian Beach?" Tim asked.

"South Carolina, I think." Emily had not been listening to the radio she had asked to hear.

William started not to say, "Indian Beach is the third one down from us." He had stood in a service station in Madison, Kentucky, and studied the names of the beaches that swam down the map: Delmont, Tompkins, Ranger, Indian. "It's the third one down," he said angrily.

Bill said, "I'll be."

Tim said, "I'm never going in the ocean again, not ever, not forever and a day. I'm not ever going to set foot in the ocean, not ever."

"That's enough," William said, glaring into the rearview mirror.

Bill jabbed his elbow into Tim's side.

"Well I'm not, and quit hitting me."

"Boys," Emily said.

Bill flounced himself into the corner of the seat. He leaned his forehead against the window. His lips moved.

"Stop that muttering," William said, and more quietly: "Speak up, if you have something to say."

Bill's face grew large in the mirror. He leaned hard against his father's shoulders. "What's a shark, I'd like to know. And now I bet you won't let us go in at all. I bet you make us go home tomorrow, just because of one little old shark." His voice cracked. His voice was almost crying. "I bet it'll be like in Florida."

Emily turned.

"I'd be ashamed," Tim said.

"Well, I mean it. It's going to be like last year in Florida."

"Bill!" Emily's knees whispered against the nylon seat covers. "Bill, I told you."

Bill was crying. A fifteen-year-old boy was crying in the back seat of the station wagon. "You won't let us go in, and who's afraid of a shark, and they won't be at our beach anyhow."

"We'll see." William's voice was as loud as if he spoke to the deaf. "We'll see. Now straighten up, there."

"We'll see, we'll see, we'll see," Bill muttered.

The words were the words of T. R. Travis. But at least T. R. Travis had pretended intimacy with his son. T. R. Travis often said, "*We'll see* means I am not capable of being a responsible law-giver. It means give me time for the situation to change so I won't have to make a decision."

William said, "I said 'We'll see.' Now, quiet, all of you." And, after a little while he said, "I'm sorry."

But the boys were arguing in low voices over how long was fifty feet: it was twice as long as their living room, it was "about out to there, no, a little bit farther," it was the length of the pool. When they turned into Ocean Side they were challenging each other on the number of pecks in a gallon.

Mr. Meigg was readying cabin number six. His scarred face chuckled as he came over to place his hand on the sill of William's window. His fingers were thin, but smooth. "Did you see the shark?" he whispered.

"We heard about it." William made himself look into the man's eyes.

Bill put his hand on William's shoulder. "Here? Was the shark here on our beach?"

"They sighted him. Just after noon." Mr. Meigg laughed at the thought. "He was a big fellow. I stood on the dunes and watched. They were after him with shotguns and clam rakes and everything. It was a sight." Mr. Meigg removed his hand from the sill to laugh and cough against his smooth fingers. "They were after him with everything. They didn't catch him, though." He was delighted with his story. "Clam rakes and shotguns, and even brooms. One old fellow had a broom."

"Really? Really?" Tim said.

"I would expect a landowner to keep this quiet." William spoke casually.

Mr. Meigg did not seem to understand. "You expect all sorts of things at the beach," he said, as if William had not spoken.

"Is there danger, of swimming, for us, I mean, for the boys?" William spoke loudly.

"Oh, I don't think so." Mr. Meigg was unable to stop smiling. "You just have to be careful. They're fast."

Emily said, "If we all go in together . . ."

"That's right. You can see them coming. They zigzag. But you can see them all right. This morning one of them chased a man clear up to the beach down at Indian, the same one, I guess."

Tim said, "It was nine feet out and fifty feet long." He giggled. "I mean the other way around."

"He just chased him right in." Mr. Meigg was giggling too, as if he were not old enough to have been wounded in a war. "The sea was quiet as a millpond, and he chased him right in."

Tim and Bill were asking questions together. William could barely distinguish their questions, but Mr. Meigg was answering the boys separately. "But you probably won't ever see one," Mr. Meigg said.

In the cabin William said, "Are they going in, Emily?" He found it difficult to think about the shark.

The boys stood at their bedroom door. They had already taken off their shirts. They held their hands at their hips; their stance was the stance of the County Snakes.

Emily lifted her hand to the lamp on the table. With the forefinger of her right hand she circled the top rim of the lampshade. She did not turn on the lamp, of course; she was beautiful in the sudden light that came from somewhere. It was the sun, of course. The sun had come out as suddenly as it had disappeared while they were talking to Mr. Meigg. William thought of other beaches where they had made love. "You're the father," she said. "You make the ocean decisions."

"Please, pretty please," Tim said. "For gosh sakes," Bill said.

"There are always sharks." William kept his voice as soft as Emily's. "We'll just have to be careful." The words were not difficult to speak. They were not nearly so difficult as saying, "We'll go back to Madison."

"Very well," Emily said. "I'll dress in the bathroom." She sounded no more pleased than if he had said, "I love you, Emily. Oh Emily, I love you."

"Oh boy," Tim said.

As he removed his clothes William thought, "Oh boy, oh boy," trying to think of Tim's pleasure. He wished to think his moment of decision into importance, at least into more importance than a moment of indecision. He was naked. He was in his bathing trunks. Tim stood at the door. "Ready, ready? Are you ready?"

"Ready," William said.

Behind Tim, Bill stood scowling through his glasses. "Why don't you leave your glasses here?" William asked.

Bill stepped back. He flipped his towel savagely against Tim's legs.

Tim whirled, yelling, "You dog, you, you . . ." His towel sailed across the room. It landed against an empty milk bottle on the drainboard. The bottle teetered before it fell to the floor. The sound of its breaking came slowly, like thunder after lightning.

Bill was shouting. "Did you see that? What are you going to do to him? If I'd a done that, I'd never hear the end of it."

"The idea. The very idea." William's fingers dug into Bill's shoulders.

"Hey. Hey, quit."

"Boys," Emily said at the bathroom door.

Bill wrenched away from William's hands. He stood at the door. "What'd I do?" He crossed his hands over his thin chest. "What'd I do to the little baby?"

"Get out. Get out of here, both of you."

"I didn't mean . . ." Tim began.

"You heard your father," Emily said softly, stooping to the broken glass.

Bill opened the screen door wide, letting it slam behind him. He stood outside and slammed it a second time before he started around the driveway.

"Bill!" William shouted.

"Leave him alone," Emily said.

"He hit me first," Tim said. "I didn't . . ."

"Go on, I said go on." William whispered.

Tim shrugged. He opened and closed the screen door with elaborate carefulness.

At the sink, in the quiet cabin, Emily turned. "That was quite a display," she said.

"I know. I'm sorry."

"You're with them so little, I would think . . ." Emily bit her lips. "You're always after them."

"I'm not always after them. It's just that . . ." He was determined to keep his voice as soft as Emily's. "I know I've been a little upset. I know . . ."

"Please, William. We don't quarrel. At least we don't quarrel."

"My God, Emily. My God."

"Please."

"A man shouldn't have to keep working things out, over and over again. You don't have to keep working things out."

She spoke so softly that William had to ask her to repeat. "That's what I mean," she said again.

"*What* do you mean?"

"Why are you afraid of the shark? Why are you afraid of the shark?" she asked, although he had heard her the first time. "No, don't touch me. No, No. *Why*?"

"I dreamed of a shark. When I was sick I dreamed of a great shark." He spoke quickly. If he spoke quickly perhaps he could say what he meant. "It's bad not to be able to tell what's real from a dream. I don't want to be sick, Emily."

"Everybody dreams." Emily leaned hard against the sink. She looked small. "No, no," she said.

"I worry about the boys, I guess." William cleared his throat. "I guess I worry about keeping us together. And about dying." He stepped back from her. "I guess I want to hold on—whatever we have."

She was moving toward him now. They were like dancers in the room. "If you had faith," she said. "If you went to church with the boys and me. If you had *faith.*"

"I try. I try, Emily."

"You didn't try. You didn't give the Church a chance, not a real chance."

"We can't talk about it. You don't want to talk about . . ."

She wore the gray suit instead of the white one. "Not if talk means going to bed together. That's what talk means to you. You've been looking at me that way. You promised. Before God you promised.

"Goddamn," he said. "Goddamn."

"William, William, William," she said. "You're right," she said. "We can't talk together. But it's all right. It's perfectly all right. You're all right."

She patted his arm before she moved around him to the door. "I'm not a bit annoyed. We're fine." She seemed to speak sincerely. Her anger had been a light switched on by mistake.

And she was right, perhaps. They were probably fine. In a few minutes it was all right to follow the road past the dunes to the crowded beach and ocean. The beach fluttered in the bright wind.

Their umbrella was already up. Emily was paying one of the blonde young men for the chair and umbrella. Bill stood tall beside her. "Here I am," Tim yelled from the edge of the water. "Here I am."

"Ready?" Emily smiled.

"I'm sorry about . . ."

Bill turned his head.

"Everything's all right. Bill's fine. Forget it," Emily said. "Now are we all ready?"

But Bill did not want to go in the ocean. "I don't feel much like it," he said. "I guess I'm catching a cold."

"We'll go in together," Emily said. "Give me your glasses. I'll put them right here in my case."

"I don't want to, I told you."

"I'll race you," William said.

"We'll rent some of those rubber rafts," Emily said.

"I said I wasn't going. Are you deaf?"

"Mister. Mister Life Guard. Wait a minute, Life Guard." Emily moved across the sand to the scarlet Jeep, opening her beach bag that was covered with round plastic suns. "Help me, Bill. Help me with these."

Emily talked well. Emily talked easily. Together they sat on the sand with the rafts for a while. Tim was delighted with his raft. "Hey, keen," he said. He raced into the water and out again. "Shark, shark, I'm a shark," Tim shouted, and the mother of the toy doll-child said, "Look at the big boy. Look at him run."

"We should of got these before."

"*Should have,*" Bill said. "It's not *should of.*"

"The water's good," Tim said. "It's just as soft and good."

"Everybody's in," Emily said. "Maybe we'll all go in after a while."

And after a while they all went into the ocean. Bill lifted both hands to his temples. He removed his glasses slowly and handed them, slowly, to his mother. "I'll just put them right in here," she said. "They'll be safe as anything."

"I can't see much without those things," Bill said. "The man said *they* slipped up on you."

How does a father say I love you? What does a man mean when he says I love you? William said, "Fine, fine."

They ran into the water together. For almost an hour they were a family with rafts near the shore. They lay on the rafts; they wrestled them; they dumped each other and themselves; they fought through the water up to air. Emily laughed a great deal. Tim shouted, "Wowie," and "Fab-O."

Once, when Bill squinted over his shoulder toward the curve of sea, William said, "I'm watching out." And Bill said, "I know you are."

The sea was a blue saucer. Gulls sailed. Sandpipers raced on tiptoes, and turned, their feathers ruffled.

"I'm cold, I'm really cold. Don't you think it's getting cold?" Bill asked.

"I think it's cold, too," Tim said. "In fact, I'm freezing to death."

"We'll get out now," Emily said.

"It's been fine," William said, his throat tight with worry or with love; and the afternoon and the evening washed quickly against him, almost too quickly to think about. "It's been very fine."

After dinner they walked by the ocean, on the beach which was charted for them now with people to nod to, with dunes and lights to recognize. The shining mother quarreled with her toy child, but the waves snatched away most of her words: "Don't you know people will . . . And don't you know you are . . ."

"Is the shark gone away?" the child whined as the Travises passed.

The mother's teeth glowed as she smiled at the Travises. "Yes, yes, darling," she said, nodding. "They killed it, darling. All the sharks are killed."

"They killed it?" Bill skipped into step beside William.

"She said so. The lady said so." Tim ran into the water until a wave splashed his shorts. "Shark, shark," he shouted, tracing numbers with his flashlight.

Far down the beach driftwood fires burned. "It's pretty, isn't it?" Emily said. "It's like a carnival, isn't it?"

The beach was full of little sharks. Almost every knot of fishermen discussed their little sharks with the people who did not fish but merely walked the beach. "Sand shark." "White shark," they told the Travises.

"Golly," Tim said. "That woman didn't tell the truth."

"A storm's blown them in," one man said; and another said they had come in because the ocean had been quiet so long.

"As a millpond," Tim said.

"But that fellow this morning—he was a whopper. Eleven feet long, anyhow."

Twelve feet, eighteen, twenty-four. He was forty feet offshore, twenty-five feet, he was in the trough of the second wave. He was last sighted at eleven; no, nearer twelve-thirty; at two. The friendly men and women and children on the beach moved together among a variety of numbers. How many people saw him? How deep is it out there? Give me a number, any number. How high is the sky?

"I bet they know about him even in Madison, Kentucky," Tim said.

"You tell 'm," a man said.

One of the twins who lived in the blue apartment house guarded the largest of the little sharks. The boy and the shark were almost the same size, three feet tall, three and a half. The boy stood the dead shark on its nose and dropped it to the sand. The boy kicked the shark. "Do it again, Charlie," his brother said.

The County Snakes had caught a hammerhead. "It's a goddam hammerhead," the boy in the red and white striped trunks said. He placed his palms on his hips.

"It's a fish," Tim said.

"Sure it's a fish." The County Snakes laughed, looking toward William.

"It's a fish, Tim," William said.

"They're killers." The boy in yellow trunks spit over his shoulder. "They smell you out."

The old lady said, "Lovely evening."

The lovely evening was very dark when the Travises returned to their dunes.

Lightning bloomed the sky a moment.

"It may rain," Emily said.

"I'm sleepy," Bill said.

"Me too." Tim yawned loudly.

"Beat you to bed."

"Oh no you won't."

At the front door William turned to study the sky a moment.

He was not Paul on the road to Damascus. He was only a man who had walked on the beach with his family.

But for a moment he was the sea. He was all of the oceans. The waters of his mind held a multitude of faces, from war and even childhood, even his mother—she was not dressed in fur: she wore a white voile dress and sat in a steamer chair, even the man at the Shell Station, his father and the boys, and Emily, Emily, Emily.

The oceans were one ocean. He considered the possibility of deafness. But he was not deaf. The wind sounded in the sky.

He did not say, "I accept the responsibility of being human." But aloud he said, "I wish you well." He spoke, perhaps, to the shark who swam somewhere, absolute, perhaps fully dark, perhaps evil. He was embarrassed at having spoken aloud.

"Goodnight, Emily," William said as she switched off the lamp above her bed. "Goodnight, boys," he said in the dark cabin.

"Don't let the bedbugs bite," Tim called over the partition.

William lay on his back, his fingers clasped behind his neck. The tent of the roof appeared and disappeared in the sudden lightning. He wondered if the flashes came at any regular intervals, but he did not consider determining their frequency by counting his own pulse, or Emily's breathing.

"We have two and a half more days." Bill's voice seemed to come from the rafters.

"I bet we can't go in tomorrow at all," Tim said.

"You can go," William said. "You may go."

"And the morning and the evening were the fifth day," William thought. He was making a kind of joke. It was a joke like "The millpond round my neck." The act of committing your family to the sea was a small act, no different, not much different from saying, "Goodnight, goodnight."

The Man from Cord's

At first she had told Malcolm every one of the experiences. "The funniest thing happened," she would begin, and Malcolm, sleek and handsome under the bridge lamp, would lower his newspaper and raise his eyebrows to listen. The paper rustled in his hands and she spoke quickly to get the experiences told. "Isn't that interesting?" she always asked at the end of the story to show Malcolm he could go back to his news.

"Weird," Malcolm said at first, and then, "Really?" and, "It happens to everybody." Finally, the night she told him about the red-haired man appearing from a bar named Cord's, just as she had known he would appear, Malcolm let his newspaper drop to the floor.

"It's happening too often, Grace, and I wish you wouldn't keep calling it an *experience*." Malcolm frowned and extended his lips as if he were summarizing a case in court. If Malcolm hadn't looked so hilariously pompous she would have burst into tears at his ugly words. "It's a *feeling, not* an experience, and you ought to get hold of yourself," Malcolm said.

"But I mean, don't you think it's a remarkable coincidence?" she asked, hoping Malcolm would not realize how much he had hurt her: she could not bear to think of the passion of his apologies. "I thought you'd be fascinated, and this afternoon, over at Mary Ellen's, I didn't tell the girls about it because I wanted to save it for you. I thought you'd be fascinated."

"You're sweet." Malcolm scratched himself and smiled, but he showed no jealousy whatsoever.

"After all, the man was positively insulting the way he looked at me, and I thought . . ." She could not be sure that Malcolm realized the significance of a bar named Cord's; yet she could hardly say to her husband as an actress could say in a play, "My maiden name was Cord; my name is Grace Cord."

"After all, Malcolm," she said, but she could not be sure that her husband was even listening. To look at him, his arms stretched towards her, the fine hair on his wrists shining golden in the light, one would not have believed he was the kind of man who scratched himself or played practical jokes.

"Aren't you going to give me a little kiss?" Malcolm Parkman asked.

"Of course," she said, twisting from his thin arms almost as soon as she was in them, hurrying back to the game room to stand, breathless, waiting for the rustle of the newspaper in the quiet house. Then she picked up her needlepoint and settled on the chaise to look at a television play she had, of course, seen before.

The girls with whom she played bridge—Mary Ellen and Frieda and Winona—were always delighted with the *experiences*. "Isn't that remarkable?" Frieda always said. And Winona, her eyes moist with sympathy, said, "Honestly, Grace, you don't mean it," and Mary Ellen, for all her neat house and well-mannered children, said, "Oh my glory," and positively wriggled with excitement. "I know, I know just what you mean," Mary Ellen said, and almost always she told some little experience which wasn't anything at all, unimportant, and dull as a dream.

"But you have the best ones," Mary Ellen said, shuffling her cards intently.

"There's surely some way to explain it," Winona said.

"It's one half of your mind being slower than the other half," Frieda said every time. "But I still don't understand."

"I bid four no trumps," Mary Ellen said, for all her graciousness.

Grace Cord Parkman nodded her head to the television screen. She had been quite right not to tell the girls about the man and Sixth Street. If one's own husband were incapable of realizing the significance of such an experience, one could not expect one's friends to understand. And a girl deserved some privacy, after all. She smiled at the television screen. After all, one had to be circumspect.

That first night she had refused to allow the man to enter her real consciousness until twenty-seven minutes after Malcolm merged with sleep, hugging his foam rubber pillow, his mouth softly open as if he were swallowing the light from the little radio beside the bed. It took admirable willpower to delay the man from Cord's, for his virility was enormous, and he positively ached to enter her mind on the bed beside Malcolm.

But she shook her head at the electric clock, and she smiled at the clock who labored to jerk the minutes from its soft white face. Her mouth formed the words, "Twenty-seven," and the number itself became a kind of experience. She was married at twenty-seven, the number of the bar must have been six two seven, and she was quite sure the red-haired man was the twenty-seventh manifestation which had come to her. "Don't hurry," she said to the clock, for her memory was rich:

She was talking to Mary Ellen on the telephone; the sun shone yellow on the table, a cigarette burned in the ash tray; "Get away from there," Mary Ellen shouted at her youngest child, and the smoke column melted to a fan.

She was looking at TIME *on the chaise; she turned the clean smelling page to see the picture of a soldier kissing his girl and a blue-jay flew suddenly into the apple blossoms outside, shaking the shadow on the soldier's trousers.*

She held her jewel box in her lap; she ran her fingers over the smooth and scratchy surfaces, stopping to feel the diamonds in her father's watch fob, and the door bell rang three short chimes.

"It was all as if it had happened before," she told the girls and Malcolm: Mary Ellen's voice and the sun and smoke; TIME and trousers and the jay and shadow; diamonds and the doorbell. "It was almost—" she extended her hands and the light caught the glass of her bracelet until it was difficult to go on with the story. "It was as if I knew what was going to happen because it had all happened before," she said, and the girls squealed with delight, and Malcolm said, "Really?"

But actually, and it was very important to be actual under the present circumstances, she had not really *known* what was going to happen until just as the experiences ceased and Malcolm began his reprehensible jokes; she had not really known what was going to happen until she stood on Sixth Street, the plated silver tureen pressed against her breast, and lifted her eyes to a bar named Cord's. Before the man from Cord's, she had known only that the experiences had happened before.

The clock jerked its twenty-seventh time, and she allowed her body to move to the corner of Maple and Sixth where she had parked her car. "This old fellow is simply a miracle worker at resilvering," Mary Ellen had said, "and he's not nearly so expensive as the people downtown."

Grace Cord had never been on Sixth Street before, on foot. That was the way she introduced the memory of the man. "I had never been on Sixth Street on foot before," her mouth said, and she switched off the radio, smiling as Malcolm, asleep, closed his mouth and swallowed. "If you're not careful, you'll miss the stop," dear Mary Ellen with her bright voice said above the clamor of her noisy children. "The number is six three four, and it's just a hole in the wall."

"It's just a hole in the wall," Grace said, and she hugged her arms tightly across her breast. Beside her a yellow cat slunk from the door of a grocery store on whose screen hung a wad of gray cotton. A stalk of green bananas almost obliterated the number, six seven three. Across the street hunched a warehouse, then the blinding sign of a Quicky Lunch, another grocery; she frowned against the sun, but the word *Plating* stood out clearly on the glass of an unpainted door. She felt quite astute for finding the number so easily when Mary Ellen, for all her cleverness and happy children, had walked the length of the block five times before she had found the shop of the miracle worker. It was hard to breathe, but only because Grace Cord had found the place so easily.

Before she turned her eyes she knew she would see two windows, half painted black, with the single word *Cord's* written in gold script in their very center, the C smoothly flourishing its long tail to underline the other letters. And just as she had expected, the door between the two black windows opened with a rush, kicked by a man's foot, and then the man himself appeared, just as she had known he would appear in his dingy white shirt with rolled sleeves and his seersucker trousers damp with sweat.

They had stood in the bright May sun looking at each other for the time it took a clock to strike noon, before the man pulled the fat black cigar from between his heavy lips and smiled. He rubbed the back of his hand across his mouth before he spoke, and the bright red hairs on his thick wrist were as heavy as grass. Mary Ellen would have turned to run; Frieda would have gasped; Winona would have wept at the words the man whispered. But Grace Cord did not even lower her eyes, even when the man with the red hair spat, even when he rolled his cigar between his lips. They stood, shadowless, held together by the sun and the reflections of their figures in the black windows, while Quicky Lunch winked its own name a dozen times. The man laughed low in his throat when she spoke to him, but he moved cumbrously to the curb, across the street, around the corner, to Oak Avenue, the damp seersucker stretched tight across his hips, the back of his shirt as wet as if he had been hosed. She had waited a long time before taking the tureen across the street, but the man had not looked back.

Even at night, twenty-seven minutes after Malcolm had gone to sleep, the man did not look back. Although his words grew so bold that one could hardly believe one's ears, although Grace Cord had to press her hands against her mouth, certain that the man would wake Malcolm, he did not look back. It was as if he mumbled, moving to the curb, "Once a night, baby, that's all," and she was unable to send her mind a second time to Maple and Sixth. But Malcolm slept, and she was grateful, and Grace was a woman of deep resources who was able to accept the fact that the other experiences had ceased.

"Those . . . those *feelings*, Malcolm, they've stopped happening," she said.

"That's my girl." Malcolm let the newspaper fold to his lap and he reached his hand toward her. His hand was dry and cold, and she knew she must never speak of the practical jokes, not to Malcolm or the girls or the man with the red hair, not so long as they all should live. "You feel good," Malcolm smiled, as if he were a kind and considerate husband.

"Let it be said to the credit of Grace Parkman," she said to herself in the game room. She had been quite clever in coping with the tricks, never once admitting by the wink of an eyelash that she was on to Malcolm. She did not really mind her husband's calling from the office twice and three times a morning to repeat the same words in the same intonations; she was not really troubled by his insistence on her rereading the articles she had read only the day before, or attending a movie she had mastered by heart. One could stop for a suit at the cleaner's over and over, or mail checks for the utilities again and again, if one were to be rewarded at night by the man with the red hair. No matter what one might say of the man from Cord's, his conversation was as comforting as it was amusing. Although his manner might be termed straightforward, he was infinitely loyal; the more Malcolm tried to confuse one, the longer the man from Cord's waited in the sun.

Winona said, "You haven't told us any of those fantastic little experiences for, weeks."

Mary Ellen said, "Darling, whatever's happened?"

"I've thought about them a lot," Frieda's large mouth said. "There's surely some explanation for it all." Frieda's gray teeth bit into a chocolate.

Grace Cord reached her hand to the lazy Susan which Winona had placed in the very center of the card table. "They don't happen any more, but . . ." She took a piece of dark fudge from the heaped lazy Susan: the bowl swung silently past her to Winona, to Frieda, to Mary Ellen; it moved very swiftly, Grace could not count the times it turned. For a moment she came close to telling the girls about the man's words and Malcolm's cruelties. But as sudden as the turn of the Susan she knew with a quiet wisdom that her husband's jokes, no matter how cruel, were merely pathetic. Poor smooth inhibited Malcolm fought against the man from Cord's; poor jealous Malcolm fought against the lewd invitations which he could only dream. Grace could pity poor Malcolm. Grace Cord was a complete human being to be greatly envied. The lazy Susan repeated itself, coming back and back. "Let's play," she said, and Winona moved the sweets to the sideboard.

The apple blossoms had turned to round sour apples when Malcolm, with feigned innocence and no earthly reason, asked, "What about that tureen, honey? Don't you guess the fellow's about finished?"

"I guess so," she said before she thought, for it was morning and the man from Cord's had lingered through the hot night beside her.

"I'll pick it up for you if you want me to."

"No, I'll get it," she said, though she had sensed all along that it was improper to return her body to Sixth Street.

It was painfully unhealthy to remember her return, but one's worst enemy would have to admit that Grace Cord had exhibited herculean control when she called for the tureen, never once allowing her eyes to move to Cord's. The plating man was really a miracle worker, just as Mary Ellen had promised, but ridiculously expensive. Grace Parkman tipped him rather liberally before she descended his steps. In all justice to the fellow he had wanted to wrap the tureen in newspapers, but she had refused in her eagerness to get away from the street. Actually, then, it was the tureen's fault that she caught its bright reflection in the black windows across the street.

If the experiences had not been cut off, if her waking mind had not been consumed with adjusting to Malcolm's evil jokes, she would not have known that Cord's Bar had changed hands. She would have been prepared for the name of the new owner, Brown, written in gold script on the black windows; she would have been prepared for the new number which crawled across the door light. But she was not prepared, and for a moment, before she ran to her car, she thought of hurling the tureen against the name, Brown. She trembled so desperately that it was difficult to insert the ignition key. She leaned her head against the steering wheel and waited for some realization to descend upon her. But she did not dream, then, that Malcolm was capable of destroying the man with the red hair.

That night, without warning, the man had disappeared. No matter how carefully she parked her mind at the corner of Sixth and Maple, no matter how many times she waited in front of the bar named Cord's, the man refused to appear. Night after night, as if in a dream, she was reduced to crawling between the black windows, throwing her body against the heavy door; when she finally succeeded in opening it a fraction, nothing emerged but a yellow cat, or the girls, or Malcolm with briefcase and homburg, even though it was summer, smiling at her, scratching delicately at himself.

She waited the twenty-seven minutes, multiplied by three and five and seven, and only morning appeared.

Malcolm rubbed the dark sleep from his face and said, "Hello, there, Grace. Have a good night's rest?"

"Yes, yes, of course," she said, avoiding his eyes.

"What's on the docket for today?"

"Nothing much." She pretended to yawn. "You?"

But of course he refused to reveal his plans, and each day the jokes became more complicated and more unbearable.

Malcolm was clever—one had to give the devil his due. Grace Cord would be the first to admit that her little husband was diabolically clever. He canceled her orders at the grocery; he cluttered the cupboards as soon as she straightened them; he destroyed a completed square of needlepoint and replaced it with new material. Doggedly she repeated everything for Malcolm, humoring him, refusing to admit, even to herself, that Malcolm was capable of destroying Grace Cord as well as the man with the red hair. Malcolm Parkman was capable of *murder.* She did not say the word aloud until the evening her body could no longer contain its loneliness.

They had finished eating: hamburgers, potato chips, tossed salad, and chocolate cake, Malcolm's favorite Sunday supper. Grace kneeled in the back yard, thinning the late zinnias she had thinned only the week before. The heat pushed so violently against her body that it was difficult to keep from falling, but she worked intently, not pausing to wipe the perspiration which seeped like tears down her face. She was suddenly conscious of Malcolm, standing at the window of the game room, but she did not look up.

"Grace," Malcolm called, making his voice sound insistent, as if he had already called a number of times.

"I'm here," she said.

"Isn't it time we were eating?"

She raised her body until it stood. He had almost tricked her into answering naturally, but she caught herself. "Of course."

Malcolm had gone to great lengths to create his joke: an unopened package of potato chips and a bakery cake were on the drainboard by the knife holder; four hamburger patties lay on the broiler rack. The little torture was so carefully contrived that she would have doubted herself if Malcolm had not made the mistake of forgetting to prepare a new salad. "I'm sorry I stayed out so long," she said carefully, moving to the stove. And, "Murder," she cried when she saw that Malcolm had turned on the oven without lighting it.

"Honey, you'll just have to be more careful." Malcolm was behind her, his thin fingers pressing into her arms. "Honey?"

"I'm sorry," she said, allowing her body to go limp against his body, proving that two would play the joke as well as one. "I'm tired, I guess I haven't been sleeping very well."

"Sweetheart," Malcolm said, and she knew with clarity, despite her weariness that there was no need to endure much longer. If Malcolm were determined to destroy her, she could accept the last joke, as she had accepted the others, for Grace Cord was a woman of great strength.

After her husband slept, she rose quietly and tiptoed to the kitchen. It was almost amusing how few ways there were to do away with human life; they had never had a gun in the house—poor Malcolm would not have known which end to use; she could not abide the thought of poison; drowning was impossible. And yet the knife set was beautifully sharp, poised and arrogant above the drainboard, as if it knew its own power and beauty. Four times within the week, at Malcolm's insistence, she had taken the set to be sharpened, not realizing that victory had lain within her patience. One could slash with the brilliant knives until there was no more blood, and Malcolm would have learned his lesson.

From the cluttered hall closet she took four bath towels and spread them softly on the kitchen floor. She raised her hands and pulled the lingering silk of her gown over her head. She stepped from her house slippers on to the dark towels which Malcolm had never cared for. "Towels should be white," Malcolm had once said, just as he had said, "I can't stand a dull knife." She smiled that she should remember such details, and that blood itself would hardly show on the dark towels.

She stretched her body six times to the holder above the drainboard, removing the lovely knives one at a time, placing them gently on the edge of the counter: "Paring knife, narrow slicer, butcher slicer, bread knife, French cook, utility knife." She named them as if they were lovers. Outside the apples were sweet and red. The moon gleamed on the apple leaves and on her breasts.

She lifted the largest knife and ran the side of its blade across her thigh as if she were a butcher.

She whispered and laughed in the kitchen.

She had already died, of course. Even this had happened before, and there wasn't any need to go through the mess again. The moon gleamed on the shining blades as she replaced them, their shadows danced against the walls.

It was an awfully interesting joke to play on poor Malcolm who needed her more than ever now that he had finally succeeded in destroying her. But she did not need to waste time in sentimentalizing. She knew, as surely as the dance of the shadows, that the man from Cord's waited for her beside the sleeping Malcolm.

The Woman Who Loved Everybody

If people said it once about Miss Nannie Louise Smith, they said it a hundred times: "Miss Nannie Louise just loves people."

Miss Nannie Louise didn't say it about herself, but sometimes she implied it, which nobody in Fayette, Kentucky, minded much, not even the very few people who didn't love Miss Nannie Louise back, not even Mrs. Sundren—Clara Sundren—or Roxie Chambers. Sometimes Miss Nannie Louise said, "It makes me tremble to think about the miracle of human life; humans are God on earth." And a lot of times she quoted a little poem:

> "There's so much good in the worst of us
> And so much bad in the best of us
> It never behooves any of us
> To talk ill of the rest of us."

If Miss Nannie Louise quoted that poem once, she quoted it a hundred thousand times.

Clara Sundren said the quote wasn't accurate, but then Mrs. Sundren never proved what was incorrect about it, even though she belonged to every book club ever founded, and she owned all the club dividends of famous quotations. The Sundren house, the mansion next door to Miss Nannie Louise's youngest brother, was absolutely lined with books. Miss Nannie Louise didn't own a lot of books, but she loved them the way she loved people; she could quote whole passages from even fiction, but she loved poetry best.

She could say "The Blessed Damozel" by heart, and she often did, for Rotary and The Twentieth Century Club; and every year she said it for the second grade because her girlhood friend, Frances Coates, taught the second grade at Fayette. Miss Nannie Louise stopped saying it for The Twentieth Century Club the year her sister-in-law played the background music so shamefully. Mattie had been accompanying Miss Nannie Louise for years and she knew the kind of music that was supposed to go with the poem, but the last time she played jazz, just plain jazz—songs like "Darkness on the Delta" and "Alexander's Ragtime Band." Miss Nannie Louise got through her performance without crying, but barely. She never said a word against Mattie, so far as anybody knew, but she refused to recite for The Twentieth Century Club ever after that, although she was a charter member, and the charter members were always on the program committee. Miss Nannie Louise was known to have said, "Forgive and forget is my motto." She implied, according to several sources, that she could forget quicker if she never said the poem again for The Twentieth Century Club. She did it without music for the second grade. And Mattie was terribly nice to Miss Nannie Louise for ever after, in her own tight mouthed way. A lot of people said that if you couldn't believe that Miss Nannie Louise really loved everybody, you couldn't believe anything.

During the flu epidemic Miss Nannie Louise made Jello in washing tubs, and her oven was never turned off. That was a long time before she moved in with Mattie and Ernest. Miss Nannie Louise never had the flu. A lot of people tried to talk to her about exposing herself. Her sister, Euba, for instance, who was living at the time and never gave anybody so much as an old buttonhook, said, "Nannie Louise, you are tempting fate, going into all those houses with all that Jello and all that gingerbread." Miss Nannie Louise said, "Love is a kind of vaccination," and she was right, at least in her case, and her sister almost died. That was when Miss Euba got the lung weakness she never did get over.

Miss Nannie Louise didn't start writing thank-you notes wholesale until she moved in with Ernest and Mattie several years after

Miss Euba died. Almost everybody except Clara Sundren told Mattie how lucky she was to have the company of Miss Nannie Louise. And even Clara Sundren admitted, when pressed, that nobody in the world made better transparent pies, or fruit cakes, or even gingerbread. But Miss Nannie Louise stopped cooking after she moved in with her baby brother. She didn't even start cooking after they made the apartment for her on the west wing of their big old house. It was a fine one-room apartment, but it crowded up fairly close to the Sundrens' wall, which made Clara Sundren furious—she wrote her son in New York that she was so furious she could absolutely kill Nannie Louise, bite her up and spit her out in little pieces. Mrs. Sundren underlined the words *kill* and *Nannie Louise* and *little* three times with her blunt pen. The story went that Colonel Sundren had asked Miss Nannie Louise to marry him before he asked Clara, and then he *had* to marry Clara. Even the son knew the story; he considered it a hilarious joke on everybody.

But Miss Nannie Louise was grateful for all that Ernest and Mattie had done for her, and she and Mattie, to all outward appearances (and what other appearances is anybody except God going to judge anybody by?) got along splendidly together. Mattie was a Tompkins and quiet, and the Smiths were always close mouthed wherever personal affairs were concerned.

When Miss Nannie Louise had company she showed off her combination stove, sink, and refrigerator, lighting the burners, running the taps, pulling out the ice cube trays. She must have shown the combination four or five times to Clara Sundren, for instance, before Mrs. Sundren said, "Yes, Nannie Louise, I know, I know, I know."

Miss Nannie Louise took everybody, even Mrs. Sundren, to the west window to admire her view of the ivy which ran up the Sundrens' serpentine walls, "designed by Thomas Jefferson," as Clara Sundren was glad to tell you. Miss Nannie Louise said ivy was her favorite foliage because it both clung and lasted and lasted. Ernest, with his own hands, after a year, built little narrow shelves on both sides of Miss Nannie Louise's fireplace so she could display her little pitchers. She said it was the first time in her entire life—even when she was living in the home place—that she had had room to display all her pitchers at once. Generally she made a kind of joke about her little pitchers having big ears. Almost everybody tried to laugh at Miss Nannie Louise's little jokes. And, of course, everybody agreed that the bay window was ideal for violets. "Look, just look at their little faces," Miss Nannie Louise said a hundred thousand times.

She started writing thank-you notes after she got fully settled in her apartment. Mrs. Sundren said that Mattie could cook as well as Nannie Louise, but she couldn't write such a pretty hand. Mrs. Sundren was glad to tell anybody why Nannie Louise stopped cooking. But most people said that Miss Nannie Louise had purely served her time cooking, what with all that Jello and gingerbread, and taking care of her parents, and Miss Euba, and raising Ernest—she was his mother for all practical purposes from the time he was ten.

She wrote her thank-you notes at the little table Ernest made for her when he was in eighth-grade Manual Training. Miss Nannie Louise treasured the table more than anything, a good bit more than the combination stove and refrigerator which must have cost five hundred dollars. Some people thought Mattie paid for the combination herself, out of her own money, though nobody knew how much money Mattie had. "Ernest made this table with love," Miss Nannie Louise said, running her hand over the surface which still wasn't exactly smooth even after all the years. "It's a little rough, yet," she said, "but it'll smooth out." Mrs. Sundren said the thank-you notes would smooth it out eventually, right down to a splinter. Miss Nannie Louise kept on writing to Mrs. Sundren, although she was bound to have heard some of the hateful things Mrs. Sundren said about her.

When people picked up Miss Nannie Louise and took her home from town, they got a thank-you note. Whoever sang in church got a thank-you note; Christmas the whole chorus got notes. Mr. Ward, the garbage collector, had quite a collection, and so did the postman, and Mr. Pullen at *The Independent Messenger.* Miss Nannie Louise's old friends, including Clara Sundren and her son who came home from New York with a disease, got the most notes. Even when they hadn't done anything, Miss Nannie Louise thanked them for just being their lovable selves, or for living in a house where the ivy "trails up a pink brick wall like a promise."

Miss Nannie Louise always did have an artistic streak. With her new apartment she had more time to herself. "Mattie is the soul of efficiency," Miss Nannie Louise said. "She doesn't really need me. I just piddle around, not helping her much. That's why I started decorating the notes."

Mr. Pullen cut tag board into card size for her. She got the envelopes from the five and dime in Lexington; and the envelopes fitted the cards like gloves, even the texture rather matched. At first Miss Nannie Louise decorated the cards with anything which happened into her mind: crayon rabbits, or a penciled silhouette of the courthouse, or a blue-ink map of Kentucky. But it wasn't long before she settled to watercolors and flowers.

After a couple of months of helter-skelter blossoms, she settled down still further to seasonal flowers in watercolors. Clara Sundren suggested that Nannie Louise's flowers had horrible significances. Mrs. Sundren remembered her mother's talking a lot about the language of flowers. "Flowers mean anything and everything, the way I remember it," she told her son. "And I think some of them mean rather terrible things such as *drop dead.*" Mrs. Sundren laughed behind her large white hand, a habit she had acquired with her new dentures; and her son turned his head. Mrs. Sundren looked for "the language of flowers" in some of her dividend books, but she couldn't find anything. She thought maybe her mother had owned a book on flowers, maybe somewhere up in the attic. But she never did locate the book, or she never looked for it. Since the Colonel's death and the return of her son from New York, Mrs. Sundren was as busy as a bird dog. She often said she was as busy as *three* bird dogs since Bunny had come home.

Miss Nannie Louise probably got wind of what Mrs. Sundren

said about the complicated meanings of her flowers, because she announced at the very next meeting of The Twentieth Century Club that her flowers were just flowers. She told everybody she was going to start being seasonal. "I hope I don't send anybody duplicates," she said sweetly. "If I should send duplicates, I hope you'll forgive an old woman's carelessness."

Two or three of the ladies said, "*Old*," and, "Honestly, Nannie Louise!" The majority of the members, except for such chits as Roxie Chambers, were Miss Nannie Louise's age and older. "You know absolutely well, we're as old as you are," Mrs. Sundren said. "Don't you ever let me hear any more of that kind of talk out of you!"

"I didn't mean to say anything bad," Miss Nannie Louise said. "But I am old. We are. Everybody *grows* old," she said, smiling around the room, even at Roxie Chambers, who was only twenty-seven.

The flowers changed from trailing arbutus, and jack-in-the-pulpits, through roses, and cosmos, to chrysanthemums and fall leaves and various evergreens, and witch-hazel, and some bare branches. Miss Nannie Louise was generally very good at keeping track of who had received what flower. Occasionally she called people on the telephone to ask if they had received the lily of the valley or the cornflower. She sounded very casual. "I just want to keep things tidy, and my notes are crisscross." Clara Sundren said, "No, I haven't received the forget-me-not, Nannie Louise. I'm sure I haven't had a forget-me-not thank-you."

Miss Nannie Louise called back in ten minutes to say she had straightened her list out. "You did have a forget-me-not, Clara. You got one for arranging the altar flowers."

Mrs. Sundren said, "Oh, Lord," but she said it away from the telephone, and Miss Nannie Louise couldn't possibly have heard her. Miss Nannie Louise didn't seem cross about Clara's forgetting what flowers she had received. In fact, she laughed about it. She said, "Clara forgot my forget-me-nots, but I forget my forget-me-nots, too, which just goes to show what kind of memories we all have."

Miss Nannie Louise's cards turned into works of art. Robert Sundren, home from New York, suggested that she sell them through some of the stores in Lexington, or Louisville, or New York even. "Go on, Robert," Miss Nannie Louise said.

Robert said, "They're like illuminated manuscripts."

Miss Nannie Louise held up the card she was working on. She said, "It's a mighty washy illuminated manuscript still. It looks as if it got caught in a pretty big rain."

"Come on, Miss Nannie Louise," Robert said, because he didn't know anything else to say. He was thinking that if the world of chance had turned a little differently, Miss Nannie Louise, who loved everybody, could have been his mother.

"You look like your Daddy," she said. "I never saw one human being favor another human being so much."

"Am I supposed to take that for a compliment?" Robert said.

"A compliment," Miss Nannie Louise said, and she started talking about her ideas for the December cards. "I'll have to have about a hundred thousand thank-yous for December. People are always terribly nice to me in December, what with Christmas and all."

Miss Nannie Louise had been mailing cards for almost a year. Mrs. Sundren said, "I'm sure it's close to a year because I've been subject to two sets of forget-me-nots. Unless Nannie Louise is lying and never sent me that first forget-me-not."

Nobody could see how Miss Nannie Louise afforded the postage. Mrs. Sundren said, "I couldn't myself even." Mrs. Sundren was not boasting. The Sundrens had more than enough money for the whole town, and they weren't likely to run out, not with their land, and investments, and inheritances—the Sundrens were always heiring money from other rich people. Miss Nannie Louise never heired anything except relatives like Miss Euba and Ernest to take care of. Ernest had done very well, of course. But Miss Nannie

Louise had no income at all, except what Ernest and Mattie slipped her from time to time. Some people wondered if she were eating properly; she was getting terribly thin.

She said she made her own breakfast; she didn't want to be in the way when Mattie was hustling Ernest off to the bank in the morning. But there never was anything in the refrigerator when she showed off the ice cube trays. Everybody assumed she ate her other meals with Ernest and Mattie, but nobody could be for sure.

Anyhow, Miss Nannie Louise stopped mailing her thank-you notes after about a year and started delivering them. Through every kind of weather, always wearing one of those crocheted scarves she fancied, she trotted all over town, slipping her envelopes in mailboxes, or under doors, or behind screen guards. After a few weeks people got on to the fact that Miss Nannie Louise preferred not to be seen delivering. If anybody saw her coming and met her at the door, she wouldn't leave the envelope; she would make some feeble excuse for being there, and then come back later. Mrs. Sundren said Nannie Louise wanted you to think the letters came from heaven.

Some people considered Miss Nannie Louise a great joke; and one or two of the young women, who had come from some place else, had no patience with her. Roxie Chambers, for instance, came from New York City, of all places. She met Cobb Chambers at the University of Kentucky and married him; and Roxie hated Fayette from the first minute she saw it. When Roxie would see Miss Nannie Louise standing at the door, fumbling an envelope out of that big old alligator bag, she would swing the door open and say, "Why, Miss Nannie Louise, whatever are you doing?" Not long ago she caught her four times in one day. Miss Nannie Louise fluttered around and made up silly excuses: "I just wanted to tell you how pretty the lawn looks," and "How's that precious baby?" and, "Could you tell me the time?" She dropped her thank-you note to Roxie, and Roxie picked it up, and Miss Nannie Louise snatched it out of her hand and stuffed it into her purse. She closed the clasp on her crocheted scarf, and she stood there fighting her purse and saying, "I wanted to remind you of church Sunday." Roxie couldn't keep from laughing in the old woman's face; but Miss Nannie Louise delivered the note that night. Roxie said, "She must have brought the goddamned letter at three o'clock in the morning. Cobb and I were already in bed, in our separate beds."

Miss Nannie Louise kept right on painting her flowers and delivering her notes thanking people for whatever it was—bearing a child, looking beautiful while walking past the post office, or having been a dutiful son to his recently deceased mother.

I am the son of the recently deceased mother.

I cannot finish this story in the phony folksy tone of a village speaker, considering a society of aging acquaintances, and church suppers, and one moving picture house, and two groceries, and The Twentieth Century Club, and a town square with a statue of Andrew Jackson, and values that nobody considers any more.

For over a year I have again lived behind the serpentine wall of the Sundrens' house. I am the artistic son who went to New York to be an actor and failed hilariously and got a disease which probably even Miss Nannie Louise knew about while she was writing me thank-you notes, decorated at first with a rabbit, "Thank you for coming home; thank you for bringing your artistic interests home to Fayette," and later with those flowers, a daffodil, and a rose, and a cosmos, and a spike of goldenrod, and a spray of cedar. "Thank you for leaving your light on late"; "Thank you for whistling past my window last night"; "Thank you, oh thank you for the magnificent new paint brush—you shouldn't have, you shouldn't have."

My notes came as often as my mother's notes came. "Oh, Lord, another one," my mother would say when the mailman brought them. She would lean against the old clock in the entrance hall downstairs and laugh large and helpless until there were tears in her eyes. "And another and another," she said, laughing against her hand while Miss Nannie Louise tiptoed off the porch, having left us leaves, and Christmas roses, and then a crocus and a willow frond.

Miss Nannie Louise loved everybody; it was the way she managed to keep on being alive. She loved all of us and her mamma and her pappa, and the sister who moved north, and Miss Euba who was wise in selfishness, and Ernest who made her a table. She loved Mattie too. She and Mattie worked out being alive together. She did not kill Mattie. I have thought a great deal about Mattie and Miss Nannie Louise.

I am trying to tell this straight.

I am tired of Gothic stories written by my kind who have returned for a little while to where they came from. I am tired of young men who are not understood by their mothers. I am tired of the promises of young men, meaning I am tired of myself, Robert Sundren, who cannot write a simple narrative about Fayette, Kentucky, and then stop writing.

I must name myself aways, Robert Sundren, who may very well be really named Bunny Sundren.

I seem incapable of letting a story stop. I know the beginning of every story is every bit as true as the ending of it; maybe it is more true because every story has to keep on beginning until the whole world stops.

Yet I am Robert Sundren. I am my kind. The ending of this part of my life is not much less true than its beginning. I think I would know this even if I were sober.

The day Miss Nannie Louise killed my mother I came up to this room and began writing about Miss Nannie Louise. I sat at this typewriter by this window. I tried to write about Miss Nannie Louise in Miss Nannie Louise's voice, but I have not even pretended to love everybody; I have written a report of what people, such as my mother and Roxie, have said about Miss Nannie Louise.

I refused to answer Ernest's knock, or Mattie's, or Dr. Gardner's, or even Roxie Chambers' who cried shamelessly outside the door and called shamelessly, "Darling, darling, please come out, please don't do anything to yourself." I did not answer any of them; particularly I did not answer Roxie. Mattie said, "Leave him alone."

She said, "Can't you leave him alone?" They left me alone, and after a while I came downstairs and went through what I was expected to go through.

That is the end of the story.

I am trying to tell this story straight without false suspense. The end of the story is that Miss Nannie Louise killed my mother. I came downstairs after my mother was dead. I do not think I heard them struggling. I think Miss Nannie Louise called me to come down. She and I looked at each other. The body of my mother was on the floor of the entrance hall. I did not have to see my mother's face; her back was toward me; I stood on the second landing. Miss Nannie Louise said, "I didn't love Clara enough." She put down the second card. She turned around and went out the door. She went next door to tell Mattie and Ernest what she had done. When Mattie and Ernest came into our hall, I went back upstairs. After a couple of hours I came out and acted the way the Sundrens have always acted, or civilized, or uncivilized, or whatever the word is. When I came downstairs my mother was no longer on the floor of the hall.

People say, "Naturally you took your mother's death hard, Bunny; you were always so close." They say, "Miss Nannie Louise just went berserk, absolutely berserk; she's been failing—all those thank-you notes." They tap their heads and lift their eyebrows and nod. They say, "You have taken it all fine, Bunny, just fine."

I have taken it all fine. I have not told the people of Fayette, Kentucky, that they lie. For all I am sure of, they have not lied. Perhaps I have done right. I would like to think I have done right, whatever the word means, as Miss Nannie Louise did right in loving everybody, whatever love means.

She could have killed Roxie as reasonably as she killed my mother. Roxie teased her on Thursday. Roxie laughed in her face on Thursday, but Miss Nannie Louise delivered her thank-you note anyhow Thursday night, thanking Roxie for looking beautiful while walking past the post office.

Friday morning I went to the Chambers' house to go to bed again with Roxie, the first time since her child was born. Friday is Co-op day in Paris, and Cobb never misses a Co-op day.

Perhaps I am incapable of telling a simple incident straight.

I do not assume that Roxie's child is also my child. I do not assume that it is Cobb's child, either. Roxie Chambers' child is not a part of this story.

After I left Roxie, Friday, about noon, I saw Miss Nannie Louise waiting for the light by the courthouse. I took her home. I got out of the car and opened the door for her. She thanked me profusely, but I knew that I would get a note. When I came into our house, my mother said, "You've been with that bitch Roxie, again, haven't you?" I refused to eat the salad or the roast beef sandwich which were waiting for me on the dining room table. My mother told Elsie, our cook, to take the roast beef sandwich over to Miss Nannie Louise.

I do not know how my mother knew about Roxie and me. That is not a part of this story. Everybody knows everything in Fayette, Kentucky, or at least a part of everything. Miss Nannie Louise knew, or she would not have telephoned Roxie, after Mattie and Ernest ran out of their house to come to our house.

Friday evening after dinner, I came up here to my room to drink from the bottle I keep in my typewriter case because my mother disapproved of drinking. I lay on my bed and looked at the ceiling. I heard my mother leave to take Elsie home. I heard my mother come back. She called me, but I did not answer. I thought of going to Roxie's again. I thought of going out into the upstairs hall and calling Roxie on the upstairs telephone. I imagined talking so loudly to Roxie on the telephone that my mother could hear downstairs, even if she had turned on the television. I imagined the words I would shout at Roxie.

It must have been nine o'clock when Miss Nannie Louise slipped up to our porch to leave one of her notes.

My mother must have gone to the door immediately. I know she did not close the door before she called to me. Miss Nannie Louise did not close the door either when she went to tell Ernest and Mattie what she had done. Friday night my mother called to me. She said, "Bunny, here's another one of Nannie Louise's crazy thank-yous. It's a thank-you for the sandwich you spit on." That is what my mother said. Her voice was very shrill. She said, "It's a crocus. Check the telephone pad up there to see if I've had a crocus before."

Miss Nannie Louise must have been on the porch with the second note she had failed to leave.

My mother's death was caused by chance, a simple moment of unintentional eavesdropping, unless my mother knew that Miss Nannie Louise was on the porch again. Perhaps my mother called to me deliberately, knowing that Miss Nannie Louise would hear. If my mother called deliberately, and I have often known her capable of such calling, my mother committed suicide.

My mother was a fat woman. Miss Nannie Louise was thinner than the willow fronds she had painted on my thank-you card for our drive up the street. "This is for you," she said after she said, "I didn't love Clara enough." She put the note to me on the little table by the clock. She took it out of her purse and put it on the table.

My mother was strong. Miss Nannie Louise was barely strong enough to lift the cover on her combination stove, refrigerator and sink. I do not think that I heard them struggling.

The world is full of impossibilities, such as love.

I am a drunk man in a locked room.

My mother was caught laughing in the face of love, as everybody has laughed in the face of love. Perhaps she was killed for love. I think my mother was caught deliberately laughing in the face of love. I would not go so far as to say that the love was Miss Nannie Louise's love for my father.

Miss Nannie Louise must have opened the aluminum storm door by herself. I do not imagine my mother opened it for her. Miss Nannie Louise must have held the crocheted scarf in her hands when she entered our hall to strangle my mother.

I do not mean to dramatize this story.

I would like to write a true sentence.

My name is Robert Sundren. I am twenty-nine years old. I have lived next door to Mattie and Ernest Smith all my life until I entered Yale University. After I came back from New York, I lived next door to Miss Nannie Louise Smith who was living with her brother Ernest and her sister-in-law Mattie.

Everybody said Miss Nannie Louise loved everybody.

Perhaps I am grateful to Miss Nannie Louise for killing my mother whom I have not loved.

I have used the word love with Roxie Chambers. I have spoken of love as if love were capable of being made in a few minutes.

I think Miss Nannie Louise loved everybody. I think she created herself by loving. I think her thank-you notes were expressions of gratefulness for other people's being alive.

I think everybody spoke as much truth about Miss Nannie Louise as people are capable of speaking.